Astrosaurs

vs

Cows In Action

The Dinosaur Moo-tants

www.**randomhousechildrens**.co.uk

Also by Steve Cole:

ASTROSAURS

Riddle of the Raptors
The Hatching Horror
The Seas of Doom
The Mind-Swap Menace
The Skies of Fear
The Space Ghosts
Day of the Dino-Droids
The Terror-Bird Trap
The Planet of Peril
The Star Pirates
The Claws of Christmas
The Sun-Snatchers
Revenge of the Fang
The Carnivore Curse
The Dreams of Dread
The Robot Raiders
The Twist of Time
The Sabre-Tooth Secret
The Forest of Evil
Earth Attack!
The T-Rex Invasion
The Castle of Frankensaur

ASTROSAURS ACADEMY

Destination: Danger!
Contest Carnage!
Terror Underground!
Jungle Horror!
Deadly Drama!
Christmas Crisis!
Volcano Invaders!
Space Kidnap!

COWS IN ACTION

The Ter-Moo-nators
The Moo-my's Curse
The Roman Moo-stery
The Wild West Moo-nster
World War Moo
The Battle for Christmoos
The Pirate Moo-tiny
The Moogic of Merlin
The Victorian Moo-ders
The Moo-lympic Games
First Cows on the Mooon
The Viking Emoo-gency

The Udderly Moo-vellous
C.I.A. Joke Book

SLIME SQUAD

The Fearsome Fists
The Toxic Teeth
The Cyber-Poos
The Supernatural Squid
The Killer Socks
The Last-Chance Chicken
The Alligator Army
The Conkering Conks

For older readers:

Z. Rex
Z. Raptor
Z. Apocalypse

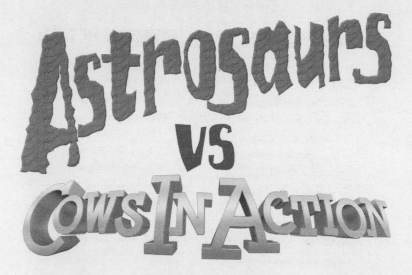

THE DINOSAUR MOO-TANTS

Steve Cole

Illustrated by Woody Fox

RED FOX

ASTROSAURS VS COWS IN ACTION
THE DINOSAUR MOO-TANTS
A RED FOX BOOK 978 1 782 95122 3

First published in Great Britain by Red Fox
an imprint of Random House Children's Publisher's UK
A Random House Group Company

This edition published 2013

1 3 5 7 9 10 8 6 4 2

The Random House Group Limited supports the Forest Stewardship Council®
(FSC®), the leading international forest-certification organisation. Our books
carrying the FSC label are printed on FSC®-certified paper. FSC is the only
forest-certification scheme supported by the leading environmental organisations,
including Greenpeace. Our paper procurement policy can be found at
www.randomhouse.co.uk/environment

MIX
Paper from
responsible sources
FSC® C016897

Set in Bembo

Random House Children's Publishers UK,
61–63 Uxbridge Road, London W5 5SA

www.**randomhousechildrens**.co.uk
www.**totallyrandombooks**.co.uk
www.**randomhouse**.co.uk

Addresses for companies within The Random House Group Limited
can be found at: www.randomhouse.co.uk/offices.htm

THE RANDOM HOUSE GROUP Limited Reg. No. 954009

A CIP catalogue record for this book is available from the British Library.

Printed and bound in Great Britain by CPI Group (UK) Ltd,
Croydon, CR0 4YY

For Florence Louise Smith

WARNING!

THINK YOU KNOW ABOUT DINOSAURS?

THINK AGAIN!

The dinosaurs . . .

Big, stupid, lumbering reptiles. Right?

All they did was eat, sleep and roar a bit. Right?

Died out millions of years ago when a big meteor struck the Earth. Right?

Wrong!

The dinosaurs weren't stupid. They may have had small brains, but they used them well. They had big thoughts and big dreams.

By the time the meteor hit, the last dinosaurs had already left Earth for ever. Some breeds had discovered how to travel through space as early as the Triassic period, and were already enjoying a new life among the stars. No one has found evidence of dinosaur technology yet. But the first fossil bones were only unearthed in 1822, and new finds are being made all the time.

The proof is out there, buried in the ground.

And the dinosaurs live on, way out in space, even now. They've settled down in a place they call the Jurassic Quadrant and over the last sixty-five million years they've gone on evolving.

The dinosaurs we'll be meeting are

part of a special group called the Dinosaur Space Service. Their job is to explore space, to go on exciting missions and to fight evil and protect the innocent!

These heroic herbivores are not just dinosaurs.

They are *astrosaurs*!

NOTE: *The following story has been translated from secret Dinosaur Space Service records. Earthling dinosaur names are used throughout, although some changes have been made for easy reading.*

THE CREW OF THE DSS SAUROPOD

**CAPTAIN
TEGGS STEGOSAUR**

ARX ORANO,
FIRST OFFICER

GIPSY SAURINE,
COMMUNICATIONS
OFFICER

IGGY TOOTH,
CHIEF ENGINEER

★ THE C.I.A. FILES ★

Cows from the present —
Fighting in the past to protect the future . . .

In the year 2550, after thousands of years of being eaten and milked, cows finally live as equals with humans in their own country of Luckyburger. But a group of evil war-loving bulls — the Fed-up Bull Institute — is not satisfied.

Using time machines and deadly ter-moo-nator agents, the F.B.I. is trying to change Earth's history. These bulls plan to enslave all humans and put savage cows in charge of the planet. Their actions threaten to plunge all cowkind into cruel and cowardly chaos . . .

The C.I.A. was set up to stop them.

However, the best agents come not from 2550 — but from the present. From a time in the early 21st century, when the first clever cows began to appear. A time when a brainy bull named Angus McMoo invented the first time machine, little realizing he would soon become the F.B.I.'s number one enemy . . .

COWS OF COURAGE — TOP SECRET FILES

PROFESSOR ANGUS MCMOO

Security rating: Bravo Moo Zero
Stand-out features: Large white squares on coat, outstanding horns
Character: Scatterbrained, inventive, plucky and keen
Likes: Hot tea, history books, gadgets
Hates: Injustice, suffering, poor-quality tea bags
Ambition: To invent the electric sundial

LITTLE BO VINE

Security rating: For your cow pies only

Stand-out features: Luminous udder (colour varies)

Character: Tough, cheeky, ready-for-anything rebel

Likes: Fashion, chewing gum, self-defence classes

Hates: Bessie Barmer, the farmer's wife

Ambition: To run her own martial arts club for farmyard animals

PAT VINE

Security rating: Licence to fill (stomach with grass)

Stand-out features: Zigzags on coat

Character: Brave, loyal and practical

Likes: Solving problems, anything Professor McMoo does

Hates: Flies not easily swished by his tail

Ambition: To find a five-leaf clover — and to survive his dangerous missions!

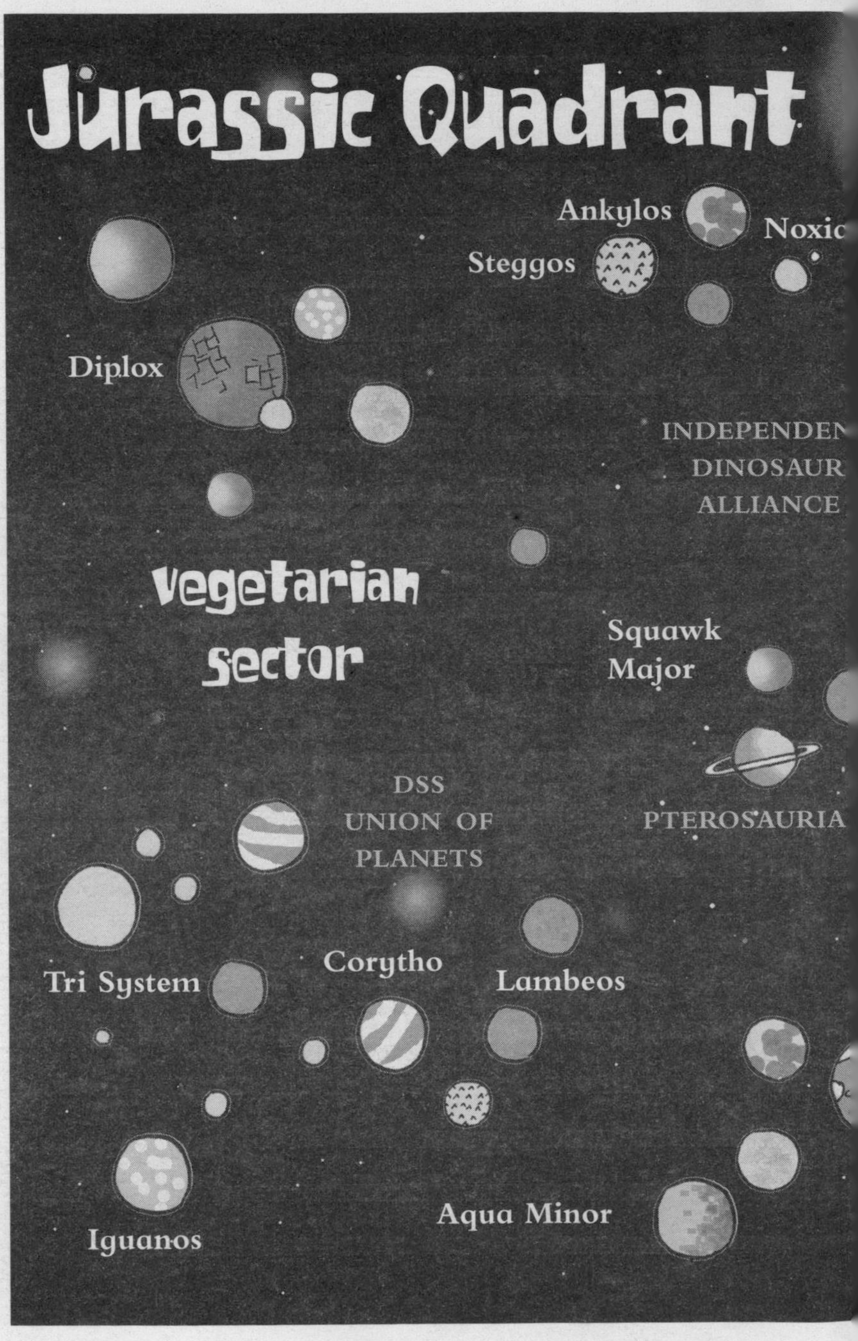

Jurassic Quadrant

Ankylos

Steggos

Noxic

Diplox

INDEPENDEN
DINOSAUR
ALLIANCE

vegetarian
sector

Squawk
Major

DSS
UNION OF
PLANETS

PTEROSAURIA

Tri System

Corytho

Lambeos

Iguanos

Aqua Minor

Geldos
Cluster

Bloodsnarl Two

Teerex
Major

Sphinx II

Olympus

TYRANNOSAUR
TERRITORIES

Planet Sixty

carnivore

sector

Raptos

THEROPOD EMPIRE

Jaggonax
Cluster

Megalos

Cryptos

vegmeat

zone

(neutral space)

SEA REPTILE
SPACE

Pliosaur
Nurseries

Not to scale

Prof. McMoo's
TIMELINE OF NOTABLE
HISTORICAL EVENTS

13.7 billion years BC
BIG BANG - UNIVERSE BEGINS
(and first tea atoms created)

4.6 billion years BC
PLANET EARTH FORMS
(good job too)

23 million years BC
FIRST COWS APPEAR

(23 million is my lucky number!)

1700 BC
SHEN NUNG MAKES FIRST CUP OF TEA
(what a hero!)

7000 BC
FIRST CATTLE KEPT ON FARMS
(Not a great year for cows)

2550 BC
GREAT PYRAMID BUILT AT GIZA
(by an Egyptian geezer)

1901 AD
QUEEN VICTORIA DIES
(she was not a-moo-sed)

31 BC
ROMAN EMPIRE FOUNDED

(Roam-Moo empire founded by a cow but no one remembers that)

1509 AD
HENRY VIII COMES TO THE THRONE

(and probably squashes it)

1066 AD
BATTLE OF HASTINGS

(but what about the Cattle of Hastings?)

1620 AD
ENGLISH PILGRIMS SETTLE IN AMERICA

(bringing with them the first cows to moo in an American accent)

1939 AD
WORLD WAR TWO BEGINS

(or World War Moo as it is known to cows)

2007 AD
I INVENT A TIME MACHINE!!!

(about time!)

2500 AD
COW NATION OF LUCKYBURGER FOUNDED

(HOORAY!)

2550 AD
COWS IN ACTION RECRUIT PROFESSOR McMOO, PAT AND BO

(and now the fun REALLY starts...)

1903 AD
FIRST TEABAGS INVENTED

Chapter One

MISSION TO PLANET SIXTY

The DSS *Sauropod* – finest spaceship in the Dinosaur Space Service – was shooting through the stars on an urgent mission.

"I *love* urgent missions," cried Captain Teggs Stegosaur, munching some leaves in his control pit. "Urgent missions mean action and adventure – and several emergency extra lunches."

Gipsy Saurine, the hadrosaur in charge of the ship's communications, had to smile. Teggs was always hungry – for exciting escapades as much as for plants! "Well, that distress call we picked

up sounded *very* urgent." She replayed the message through the speakers.

"*Attention all astrosaurs!*" came a booming voice. "*We have crashed on Planet Sixty . . . Immediate help needed! PLEASE!*"

The ship's pterosaur crew – fifty frantic dimorphodon – had flapped into furious action the moment the message came through. Now Sprite, their leader, directed them about the flight deck as they worked the ship's smaller controls with beaks and claws.

"I wonder who sent that distress call," mused Arx Orano. He was a brainy green triceratops, and Teggs's second-in-command. "Planet Sixty's in the Vegmeat Zone. No ships that we know of were flying anywhere near there – it's too

close to carnivore space. It might be a trap."

Teggs nodded thoughtfully. "The last time we visited Planet Sixty, there were T. rexes *and* raptors running about. Iggy and I barely escaped with our lives."

"Did somebody say my name?" Iggy Tooth breezed onto the flight deck, a greasy spanner in his hand. He was the *Sauropod*'s tough chief engineer, and very handy in a tight spot. "I've just got Shuttle Alpha ready to go. What's all the rush?"

"We've just picked up an urgent distress call," Teggs explained. "We're on our way to—"

"Planet Sixty?" Iggy groaned as he spied the brown blob approaching on the scanner screen. "Not that dump! I thought it was a T. rex world now . . . ?"

Arx shook his head. "It's such a rubbish place, even the T. rexes gave up on it. It's been abandoned for over a year."

"Or so we thought." Teggs gulped down some more ferns and jumped out of the control pit. "All right, team – put on your battle armour and let's hit the shuttle. Sprite, you're in charge until we get back."

Sprite saluted with both wings. "Ker-chup!"

Soon, the astrosaurs, clad in their protective gear, were bundling aboard

4

the shuttle. Teggs wore his head armour, and his tough tail was made mightier still with electro-spikes. Iggy had put on his stun claws. Arx wore his battle helmet, and Gipsy's blue combat suit covered her from tail to hooves.

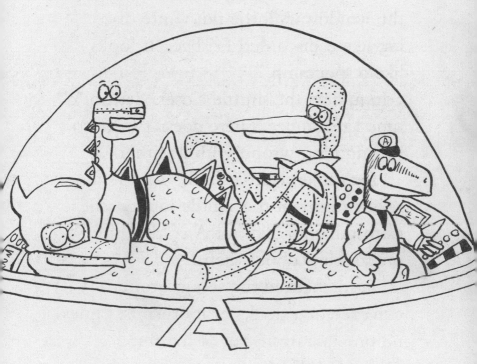

"We're good to go and ready for anything," Teggs declared. "Iggy — take us down to Planet Sixty!"

The shuttle's twin jet thrusters burned brightly. Seconds later, they were scorching through the planet's grotty green atmosphere.

"I see something!" Gipsy pointed down at the swampy ground through the window. A large flat white disc lay like a discarded Frisbee. "It looks like a spaceship."

Iggy flew the shuttle closer. "It's not a type I recognize. There doesn't seem to be anything wrong with it, either."

"Let's take a closer look," said Teggs.

The moment the shuttle landed, the astrosaurs hurried out. A cold, whiffy breeze blew about them.

Gipsy checked the soggy ground. "I can't see any tracks or footprints. I guess no one has come out of the ship."

HUMMMM. Even as Gipsy spoke, a ramp began to lower from its side.

"Whoever's on board has been waiting for us," Teggs realized, going closer.

"Hello?" he called. "Did you send a distress call? Are you OK?"

Moments later, a massive figure appeared at the top of the ramp. Teggs gulped and backed away. It could have been a T. rex had it not been for the huge white horns sticking out on either side of its scaly head . . . the long, swishing tail with fur at the end . . . and the large pink wobbly blob sticking out of its tum. It gazed around, opened its fearsome jaws and let rip with a deep, bone-trembling "MOOOOOOOO!"

Then, ignoring the astrosaurs, the creature stamped down the ramp, bent over and started to chew some swampy grass.

"A carnivore that eats grass?" Teggs wondered warily.

"What *is* that thing?"

"Me am *C. rex!*" the bizarre
beast grunted. "C. rex short for . . .
Tyrannosaurus Cow!"

"Or 'cow-rex'?" Arx suggested. "You
know, like a T. rex crossed with a cow?"

"Oh. Yeah," said the C. rex. "That
be it."

Iggy looked blank. "What's a cow?"

"A grass-
eating animal
that evolved on
Earth long
after we dinos
moved away,"
explained
Gipsy. "I read
about them in
a galactic science
book. That wobbly-
bobbly pink thing is an *udder*, I think.
Cows make milk in them to give to
their babies."

"All T. rexes give their babies is a dead rat and a bite on the bum," Arx noted. "Maybe this creature is kinder."

Teggs was puzzled. "But our long-range mega-scopes show that Earthling spacecraft are primitive compared to ours. How could a cow reach the Jurassic Quadrant?"

Suddenly, the C. rex reared up. "Ugh!" It spat out its green meal. "Me hopes grass gonna taste better with RAW MEAT . . ." Jaws opening wide, the monster stomped towards the astrosaurs.

"Battle stations, everyone!" Teggs cried. He curled into a spiky ball and hurled himself at the thing's legs.

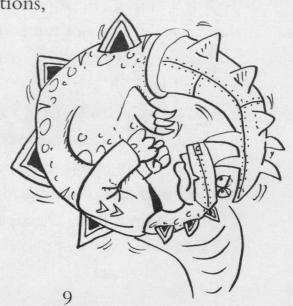

THUMP! The C. rex tripped over and fell flat on its snout.

But before the other astrosaurs could grab it, the monster rolled over and fired a sizzling spray from its udder.

"Arrrgh!" Teggs cried as his skin steamed in the downpour. "That's not milk . . ."

The C. rex grinned and nodded. "It be stomach acid!"

"Gross!" Teggs hurled himself clear of the udder attack, cooling his burned skin in a big swampy puddle. "Gipsy!" he shouted. "Signal the *Sauropod* and get reinforcements!"

"I'm on it," she called, rushing back to the shuttle.

Arx lowered his horns. "I think it's time we taught this thing a lesson."

"That's a *stunning* idea!" said Iggy. He raised his special claws, and blue crackles of energy fired from the tips.

The C. rex was stopped for a moment

by the electric onslaught. Arx charged,
aiming for its udder. But at the last
moment the monster grabbed him round
the neck with its long tail. It spun him
round and threw him at Iggy – just
as the iguanodon fired a second time.
ZZZAPPPP! Both astrosaurs were
engulfed in the stunning sparks
and collapsed on the ground.

"Oh no!" Teggs rushed across to check on his fallen friends. "Arx! Iggy!" Their eyes were closed, and they were hardly breathing. "Hang in there, guys," he said, using his spiky tail to drag his crew mates towards Shuttle Alpha. "I'll get you out of here."

"Ha!" snarled the C. rex, pounding towards him. "Not if me gets you first."

But then Gipsy bounded back out of the shuttle, a speeding blur. "Keep going, Captain! I'll buy you some time." She launched herself into a flying jump-kick . . .

Unfortunately, the C. rex lowered its hugely horned head and butted her in mid-air – *WHUMP!*

"Yeooowwwww!" Gipsy flew straight over Teggs and smashed into the side of the shuttle.

"Gipsy!" Teggs cried. He hurried across to where she lay face-down in the dirt. A big bump had come up on the back of her head.

"Now *she's* out cold too!" Teggs quickly heaved her aboard the shuttle, doing the same for Iggy and Arx. "I only hope reinforcements are on the way . . ."

He trailed off as another figure strode down the flying saucer's ramp to stand beside the snarling C. rex. It looked like a robotic cow encased in armour, walking on mechanical hind legs, with glowing green eyes and jagged metal horns. Its snout was pierced by a silver ring. *T-5* was stamped on the golden breastplate.

"Not a bad start." The creature patted the C. rex on the back. "Well done."

Teggs flexed his tail in warning. "I don't know who you are," he began, "but if that thing's your pet, you should keep it under control."

"The dinosaur moo-tant is not a pet. It is a weapon." The creature smiled evilly. "I am TER-MOO-NATOR T-5. I serve the Fed-up Bull Institute – a master race of conquering cattle from the planet Earth. We intend to dominate the galaxy – and NOTHING will stand in our way!"

Chapter Two

THE VANISHING ENEMY

"Spare me the power-mad gloating."
Teggs stared, astonished, at the ter-moo-
nator. "Conquering cattle? I thought those
funny human things ruled the Earth?"

"Humans? *Poo*-mans more like," sneered
T-5. "They are inferior and will be
destroyed – once our work here in space
is done." He pulled a long-barrelled gun
from inside his armour and passed it to
the C. rex. "It is time for weapons training
– with the butter-bazooka."

"I don't like the sound of that," said
Teggs, "and I'm sick of the sight of you
two!" As blistering yellow goo burst out
of the bazooka, he threw himself forward,

skidding on his belly, dodging the blast. Then he brought down his tail with astonishing force. As it struck the soggy ground, a terrific explosion of mucky marsh-water splashed over the C. rex and the ter-moo-nator, blinding and choking them. Seizing the advantage, Teggs shoulder-charged the spluttering pair, knocking them to the ground.

At the same moment, two egg-shaped ships came swooping out of the sky.

They unleashed a
volley of laser
bolts and dung
torpedoes at
the flying
saucer,

which
smoked and shook.
"The *Sauropod's*
shuttles," Teggs cheered.
"Just in time!"
But while Teggs was
distracted, the C. rex clobbered
him on the head with the butter-
bazooka. "*Oof!*" Teggs fell
backwards with a
splash.

The ter-moo-nator snatched back the gun. "Combat test completed," he said without emotion. "Retreat."

Teggs scrambled up to find T-5 and the C. rex vanishing up their ramp, which closed behind them. Within moments, the saucer from Earth was whooshing away, with the little ships chasing after.

Teggs rushed back to his shuttle, where Iggy, Arx and Gipsy were starting to stir.

"That *cow*-nivore kicked our butts," said Iggy, rubbing his head. "Did it get away?"

"Yes, together with its metal-brained boss. The shuttles have gone after that flying saucer." Teggs jumped aboard. "Right now, I'd better get you three to the *Sauropod* sick bay." He started up the engines and gripped the steering stick. "Hold on tight!"

The astrosaurs were soon being checked out by dino doctors. Gipsy's head was bandaged, and Arx and Iggy were given anti-stun pills. A pterosaur nurse rubbed soothing cream over Teggs's acid burns.

Suddenly, Teggs's communicator bleeped. "*This is Security Chief Alass, calling from Shuttle Beta.*"

Teggs leaped off his sick bed, giving his nurse a fright. "What's happening, Alass?" Alass Tikka was a gruff, tough ankylosaur; she was very useful in a fight. "Did you manage to stop that saucer?"

"*Sorry, Captain. It got away.*" Alass sounded furious. "*It was too fast for us. Its jets are very different from ours.*"

"All right, Alass, back you come. Tell Shuttle Gamma to return too." Teggs sighed and switched off the communicator. "We must find the dinosaur moo-tant and his metal mate – *and* their mysterious masters."

Gipsy nodded, rubbing her head. "They're way too dangerous to be left on the loose."

"Too right," growled Iggy. "Besides, I need to pay them back for making me zap poor Arx like that."

"Well, we won't find them hanging around here." Teggs stalked out of the sick bay, with Arx, Iggy and Gipsy close behind. "Let's get back to the flight deck."

The lift took them straight there. Sprite the dimorphodon flapped out of the control pit as Teggs approached. "Erp!" he said.

"Admiral Rosso wants to speak to us?" Teggs smiled; Rosso was the bespectacled barosaurus in charge of the DSS. "Well, I want to speak to him too! Put him through, Gipsy."

Gipsy pressed some buttons, and the image of a large green dinosaur appeared on the scanner.

"Ah, Teggs," Rosso began, nodding as the astrosaurs saluted. "I need your help with a mysterious robbery. One thousand tons of long grass have been stolen from Mossmunch II—"

"Sorry, sir, but we've just stumbled on something more important," said Teggs. "Answering a bogus distress call, we ran into a robot bull from the planet Earth whose masters are planning galactic domination."

Arx nodded. "They're crossing cows with T. rexes to create dinosaur moo-tants."

Rosso's eyes bulged behind his glasses. "Well, that does sound a bit more important, I admit. Tell me more . . ."

The astrosaurs gave Rosso the whole story.

"Before he left, T-5 said, 'Combat test complete'," Teggs concluded. "He wants galactic domination. He must be planning some kind of attack."

Gipsy nodded. "We must find him *and* his Fed-up Bull Institute bosses – and stop them."

"I will ask all DSS ships to keep their eyes peeled for that saucer," said Rosso. "And if I hear anything else about dinosaur moo-tants I'll let you know. Keep in touch. Rosso out."

The crusty old barosaurus faded from the screen.

"I just thought of something," said Iggy. "Alass said the flying saucer's jet engines were very different from ours. That might mean they've left a trail through space behind them . . . A trail we can follow!"

"Of course!" Arx beamed. "I'll check

all frequencies on the space scanners."

"Good thinking, Arx," said Teggs. "Gipsy, you and the dimorphodon must check all space messages – keep an ear out for any saucer sightings in the Carnivore Sector as well as here. And Iggy, you'd better stoke the ship's engines with the nastiest dung you can find – the moment we spot that moo-tant spacecraft, I want to be hot on its trail."

Iggy smiled grimly. "Those curried pineapples we had for breakfast will do the job."

As his friends saluted and began their work, Teggs sank down in his control pit and chewed on a small bush. "There's a mega-mystery brewing here," he muttered, "and it's down to the astrosaurs to get to the bottom of it!"

Chapter Three

THE JAWS OF DEATH

On the other side of the galaxy, three very different cow-creatures were speeding through infinity. Not in a flying saucer, but in a U.F.O. . . .
An Unidentified Falling-apart Object! It was unidentified simply because no one could see it flying through

the impossible vortex of past, present and future. And while it looked like a ramshackle old cowshed that might collapse at any moment, it was in fact a super-special time machine – the incredible creation of one brilliantly brainy bull . . .

"Twenty-sixth century, here we come!" Professor Angus McMoo galloped around the control panel in the centre of his Time Shed, flicking switches as he went. "I can't wait to pick up some more of those amazing future tea bags, mmmmm . . ."

Pat Vine, a young brown bullock, smiled. "Looks like the professor's already got through those Chinese tea bags we picked up last week in the twentieth century."

Little Bo, Pat's milk-cow big sister, yawned. "*And* the half-ton of Indian tea leaves from the sixth century we got the week before." She sighed. "We've turned into time-travelling tea-tourists! I wish the C.I.A. would send us on another mission."

"It's been a month since the last one," Pat agreed. While he liked living on a quiet organic farm – and loved touring history with the professor – he was missing their incredible adventures with the Cows In Action.

This group of advanced time-travelling spy-cattle from the year 2550 had made the professor, Pat and Bo their star agents – even though they lived over five hundred years in the past. For McMoo and his young friends were no ordinary cows. They were the first of a special breed of Clever Cattle who would one day grow smarter than human beings – and for some time now they'd been fighting evil bulls from the future all across history . . .

"Perhaps we've foiled the Fed-up Bull Institute's plans so often, they've given up," said Pat. "They must know we'll never let them mess up human history and put savage cows in charge of Earth."

"Miserable quitters!" Bo blew a large gum bubble. "How am I meant to get my fill of punching losers if they go and give up like a bunch of babies?"

Pat rolled his eyes. Unlike him, Little Bo was a feisty rebel whose idea of fun was getting into fights and painting her udder unusual colours (today it was blue and green).

Suddenly, the Time Shed rattled.

"We're here!" McMoo announced. "The future cow paradise of Luckyburger in the year 2550. I've put us down in the grounds of the Palace of Great Moos."

"But that's the C.I.A.'s headquarters!" Pat smiled knowingly. "Professor, you wouldn't be thinking of dropping in to see if there's a mission for us . . . ?"

"Me? No! I just love those big buckets of tea they sell in the canteen." McMoo winked. "Although, while we're here, it might be an idea, mightn't it? A bull cannot live by tea alone! He needs some action too."

"So does this cow," said Bo, kicking open the Time Shed's doors. "So let's go and grab some."

She charged off outside . . .

But two seconds later, she dashed back, her rosy hide pale and her udder quivering.

"What's up?" asked Pat, puzzled.

"We're not the only visitors from the past here today," said Bo breathlessly. "Look!"

From outside there came a terrifying roar. McMoo crossed to the door with Pat – and both cows gasped in shock.

Pounding towards them across the perfect gardens of C.I.A. HQ was a gigantic sharp-toothed *dinosaur* – dressed in ragged green clothing! Frozen with horror, Pat could only stare as the prehistoric beast stamped ever closer – its meaty butt swinging from side to side, its drooling jaws open, ready to crunch down on cow- flesh . . .

"Remarkable!" Professor McMoo clapped his hooves with delight. "Pat, I think that's a torvosaurus from the Jurassic period – related to the megalosaurus. Bones discovered in the 1970s, I believe. I don't know about the outfit, but—"

"Professor!" Pat squeaked as the giant beast lumbered closer. "Now we know what it is, can we try hiding from it?"

"Ah, yes," said McMoo. "Good thinking. Although a torvosaurus does have an amazing sense of smell and will obviously find us almost immediately—"

"Look out!" bellowed Bo from the Time Shed.

"Yep, noticed the big dinosaur, thanks!" Pat told her.

"I mean, look out for *this*!" Bo staggered out with the Time Shed's costume cupboard, stuffed full of outfits from all ages for use on C.I.A. missions. "This dinosaur obviously likes dressing up, so . . ."

As the prehistoric giant lunged forward to chow down on the cows, Bo jammed the end of the wardrobe between its jaws. *KER-CRUNCH!* The heavy wood broke apart and costumes spilled out into its mouth. A monk's robes, a suit of armour, even an enormous pair of pants, all got stuck in the dinosaur's teeth. The torvosaurus turned away, spitting and coughing and clawing at its overstuffed jaws.

"Nice going, Bo!" Professor McMoo beamed.

"Yes, thanks, sis." Pat's legs felt so wobbly he almost fell over. "But what's going on? Where did that thing come from?"

Suddenly, out of the bushes rushed a herd of bulls and cows, all wearing dark

31

glasses and purple sashes. The ones in front fired strange-looking guns at the dinosaur. Thick cables burst out and turned into heavy steel nets that wrapped themselves around the scaly giant. The nets glowed blue, and at once the dinosaur stopped struggling and toppled to the ground.

"Sorry about that, troops. The sleep-o-nets should keep this thing down now." A large black bull with curly horns and the biggest sash of all strode up to McMoo, Pat and Bo. "We had it locked up, but it got out and made a run for it."

"Yak!" The professor shook hooves heartily with the burly bull. "How's the Director of the Cows In Action today?"

Bo gave Yak a hug. "Feeling a little dino-*sore*, Yakky-baby?"

"This dressed-up brute was delivered to the Palace of Great Moos in an enormous crate," Yak growled. "It almost ate a dozen agents before we got it under control and locked it in a cage."

"So how did it get out?" Pat wondered.

"It picked the lock of the cage with its longest claw." Yak nodded gravely. "It seems the dinosaurs were a whole lot smarter than we thought."

"They died out sixty-five million years ago," McMoo mused. "The Time

33

Shed doesn't have the power to go back that far."

"Nor do C.I.A. or F.B.I. time machines," Yak admitted. "Where it came from is a total mystery . . ." He pulled out an envelope from his sash. "Anyway, we found this note in the crate." Yak handed Pat a piece of paper. "It's bad news."

With a feeling of quivering doom, Pat read it aloud:

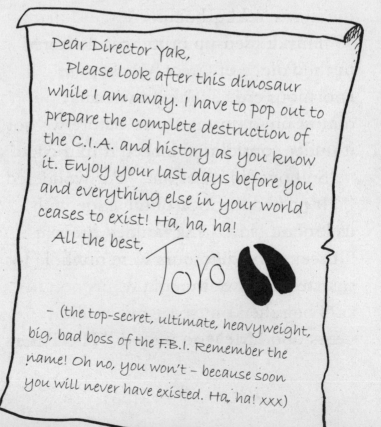

Dear Director Yak,
    Please look after this dinosaur while I am away. I have to pop out to prepare the complete destruction of the C.I.A. and history as you know it. Enjoy your last days before you and everything else in your world ceases to exist! Ha, ha, ha!
    All the best,
    Toyo

    – (the top-secret, ultimate, heavyweight, big, bad boss of the F.B.I. Remember the name! Oh no, you won't – because soon you will never have existed. Ha, ha! xxx)

Chapter Four

ASSIGNMENT: OUTER SPACE!

"Toro, the head of the F.B.I . . ." Pat breathed. "Yak, is that true?"

"So it seems," the director said grimly. "The true identity of the F.B.I.'s leader has always been their best-kept secret. But now Toro's simply come out and told us."

"Why would he do that?" said Bo. "Is he a dur-brain?"

"More likely, he's feeling very confident," McMoo murmured. "Toro is up to something very clever and probably very nasty, and wants you to know about it."

Bo raised her front hooves. "He'll know

about *these* when I clobber him!"

"Come with me, troops," said Yak, "and I'll tell you what we've discovered so far . . ."

As he led the way across the churned-up gardens, the torvosaurus stirred beneath the net and shook its

hindquarters, growling and grumbling. Pat shivered. He had the strangest feeling that the dinosaur from who-knew-where was trying to *talk* to them.

But that was impossible. Dinosaurs — even dressed-up ones — were just stupid animals.

Weren't they?

"To tell you the truth," Yak began, "we thought the F.B.I. had given up. Our time scanners couldn't find the tiniest trace of them visiting the past. But one day we looked ahead in time instead . . . and found that F.B.I. agents had been travelling into the *future*."

"Huh?" McMoo frowned. "But they've always wanted to change history and make cows the top dogs in place of humans – if you'll pardon so many mammals in one sentence. What can these F.B.I. agents be after?"

"They've been stealing the designs for super-advanced human spaceships that won't be invented for thousands of years," Yak explained, "along with the parts and equipment they need to build one of their own."

McMoo raised his eyebrows. "So the F.B.I. are going into space?"

"Good riddance!" said Bo.

"They're not just giving up and leaving the planet," said Yak. "They're planning something – far away, on the other side of the galaxy." He led the way towards a small arch in a towering hedge. "Their spaceship looks like a flying saucer. It's powered by cosmic rays and can zip through the universe at one hundred times the speed of light."

"Impossible!" McMoo spluttered. "Nothing moves that quickly – not even *me* when there's a cuppa on offer." He stopped and looked meaningfully at Yak. "Speaking of which, I don't suppose . . . ?"

"*Yes!*" Just then, a young ox rushed up, carrying a large wooden box, an envelope and a metal pail full of tea. "Here's a new tea for you to sample, Professor."

"Ugh!" Bo grimaced. "That stuff stinks like a dredged pond."

"It's called Plurge," the ox told her primly.

38

"In this century, it's the most prized tea in the world. It's made with a special herb recently discovered in the Amazon rainforest that is supposed to have special medicinal properties . . ."

"Proper *teas* — that's all I'm bothered about!" The professor drained his bucket in one gulp. "Ahhh! Not bad at all. Got any more?"

"We thought you might ask." The ox smiled and presented McMoo with the box. "Here are one hundred Plurge tea bags for you."

"Do they come with one hundred clothes pegs to stick on our noses?" asked Pat hopefully.

"No," said the ox. He handed the envelope to Yak and saluted. "This is for you, Director, from the technical department."

"Aha!" Yak pulled out a plastic card and studied it. "We've managed to track the F.B.I. flying saucer to a distant asteroid."

"Wow!" McMoo tossed the empty tea-bucket over his shoulder – hitting the poor ox on the head. "If only we could follow them there, all that way through space. Imagine that!"

"As it happens, you *can* follow them there." Yak led the way through the gap in the hedge and smiled. "We were about to call you over; after that business with the moon landings in 1969, you three are my only agents with space combat experience. So . . ."

Pat, Bo and McMoo gasped in perfect unison. There, in the middle of the ornamental lawn, stood an enormous flying saucer!

"Toro left behind his how-to-build-a-saucer plans and equipment in a known F.B.I. hideout," Yak explained, "so we decided to build our own."

"That was careless of him," said McMoo thoughtfully. "I'd expect better from the head of the F.B.I."

"You can tell him off when you find him." Yak handed McMoo the plastic card. "Slot this into the computer and the saucer will home in on Toro's ship. What happens after that . . . we don't know." He lowered his voice. "Toro wouldn't go to all this trouble just for a joyride. Whatever he's up to, it's got to be big, bad and very, very dangerous. So, if you'd rather sit this one out and go back to the farm, guys, that's cool."

"Cool?" McMoo grinned. "Why settle for 'cool' when you can have proper 'cold' – 270 degrees below freezing in the vastness of space? I'm up for it!"

"Me too!" whooped Bo.

"You'll find spacesuits hanging up inside," said Yak with a little smile. "The instruction book's in the glove compartment but everything has been pre-programmed – press the green button and you'll be away."

"Er, are you sure, Yak?" asked Pat. "Have you tested that thing yet?"

"'Cos if you haven't, we'll do it for you! Won't we, Pat?" Bo ushered the young bullock inside the gleaming white craft. "Oooh, I love flying new machines . . ."

"Moovellous!" McMoo grinned and tapped his box of tea bags. "I only wish you had a flying *teacup* to go with the saucer – mmmm, a *Brew*-F.O. . . . . what a tea-licious treat that would be!"

Yak watched the professor follow Pat and Bo inside the spaceship. "Whatever you find up there, troops," he murmured, "good luck!"

Five minutes later, the saucer trembled,

then shook, and finally took off in
a haze of light. In the swish of a
tail, it had vanished from sight.

Into the unknown . . .

Chapter Five

PERIL ON JAGGONAX

Back in the Jurassic Quadrant, a very impatient Teggs was pacing up and down the *Sauropod*'s flight deck. He'd been pacing for so long, he was starting to leave dents in the floor!

His crew were working hard. Gipsy was checking space transmissions for any clue to T-5 and cow-dino's whereabouts. Iggy was stoking the engines, ready for a fast getaway. And Arx . . .

"Arx, any luck picking up the trail of that saucer?" Teggs asked, for the 232nd time.

"Not yet, Captain," said Arx, also for the 232nd time.

Gipsy suddenly sat up bolt upright and pulled off her headphones. "Captain, I've just heard something!"

Teggs bounced in the air. "You know where the saucer has gone?"

"Um, no," Gipsy admitted as Teggs flopped down again in disappointment. "But listen to this transmission I picked up from the Tyrannosaur Territories . . ." She pressed a button and a deep growly voice came out of the ship's speakers:

"*This is a 'missing carnivore' message . . . There is still no trace of the torvosaurus space*

45

ambassador, *Cindy P. Bumbum,* who was
kidnapped last month during a visit to the
*Vegmeat Zone. Eyewitnesses say she was
pushed into a flying saucer by a robot with
horns. No one has seen or heard of her since,
or reported her as eaten. But if she was
eaten, please would the eater say sorry.
And, er, tell us if she tasted nice."*

"Sounds like she was taken by T-5,"
Teggs realized. "So these cattle-warriors
have attacked carnivores as
well as plant-eaters—"

"I'VE DONE IT!" boomed
Arx, sending a flock of

dimorphodon
scattering in
alarm. "I've
found a
faint trail
of ultra-
light atoms,
leading away

from Planet Sixty and heading towards the Jaggonax Cluster, higher up in the Vegmeat Zone."

"I remember Jaggonax!" Teggs cast his mind back. "Once it was a sunny little planet. Carnivore miners moved in, split it apart, then took out all the precious minerals."

Arx nodded. "It's abandoned now."

"By dinosaurs, yes. But perhaps not by dinosaur moo-tants . . ." Teggs leaped into the control pit and spoke into his communicator. "Iggy, stand by to boost the engines. We're going after that flying saucer. And this time, we won't let those cow-creeps get away!"

At that very moment, the experimental saucer with the Cows In Action on board was zooming towards the Jurassic Quadrant. It darted about like a deranged tadpole, blazing a path through the strange infinity of outer space.

In the bright, white control room, held in their seats by gravity straps, McMoo, Pat and Bo watched stars and planets whistle past the windscreen at mind-staggering speeds. The engines howled. Flight computers hissed and whirred. The two fluffy dice hanging from the rear scanner shook slightly.

"Wheeeeee!" yelled Bo, holding her front legs above her head like a human on a roller-coaster. "How fast are we going? About a hundred miles an hour?"

McMoo shook his head. "Try 29 billion, 979 million, 246 thousand miles per *second*!"

"I wasn't far off then," said Bo.
"WHEEEE-EEEEE!"

Pat groaned as his stomach flipped and flollopped. "How long will this journey take?"

"*Pre-programmed flight pattern almost complete,*" said the celestial sat-nav in a calm, computerized voice. "*We will be landing in point-zero-one-two of a second.*"

"Huh?" Pat gasped.

WHUMPPP!

The saucer stopped
with a sudden bump.
The engines cut
out. The gravity
straps snapped off
and the C.I.A. agents
slid out of their chairs.

"*You have reached your destination,*" said the sat-nav. "*Have a nice day in outer space.*"

"Ta, gadget!" said Bo, stretching. "It's good to be able to moooove again. I thought the journey would never end."

"It only took about twenty minutes!" said McMoo in disbelief. "This spacecraft is *incredibly* advanced!" He picked up some tea bags from the box the ox had given him. "I bet it even makes a nice cuppa for you!"

"*No,*" said the sat-nav.

"No?" McMoo crossly shoved the  tea bags into his spacesuit. "I take it back – this saucer is rubbish!"

"I'm just glad it got us here in one piece," Pat said shakily. He felt a long, long, *long* way from home. "But where *is* here?"

"*You have landed on one of the rocks that make up the Jaggonax Cluster,*" said the sat-nav. "*An identical flying saucer is parked outside, next to an old space mining base.*"

"If an identical saucer is outside, it can only mean one thing," said McMoo, putting on his space helmet. "Toro is here."

"Unless this is actually a service station for any old flying saucer!" Bo frowned. "Hang on — we haven't got our special nose-rings. If we meet any aliens, we won't be able to understand them."

McMoo shook his head. "The C.I.A.'s ringblenders wouldn't work anyway — not out here. They translate cow-speak into any human language and back again — but who knows *what* they speak in outer space."

Pat shivered. "There could be anything waiting for us out there . . ."

"Don't worry, little bruv." Little Bo patted his shoulder. "We've already met a dinosaur today — and it can't be anything crazier than that, can it . . . ?"

Putting on their space helmets, Pat and Bo followed the professor out of the saucer.

They found themselves in freezing darkness. Pat felt tiny next to the vastness of the starry sky all about him. To his right was the F.B.I. saucer, and straight ahead was a huge, white plastic dome, glittering in the icy starlight.

Wasting no time, the professor approached the plain white door of the mining base and stuck a screwdriver into the controls. Within seconds, the door was sliding open to reveal a bare, dimly lit space beyond.

"Lousy security," said McMoo. "Come on, let's make the most of it. If Toro is in, we'll give him a big surprise."

"A big punch, you mean!" said Bo.

The cattle stepped inside and the door closed behind them. Quietly, carefully, the three friends crept through the gloomy, silent corridors of the space base. It seemed deserted.

"There's a door here, Prof," whispered Bo, nodding to a large metal hatch in the wall. "Can you do your screwdriver trick and force it open?"

But then the door slid open of its own accord — to reveal a massive, menacing metallic bull with glowing green eyes.

"A ter-moo-nator!" Pat gasped.

At once, Bo threw a punch, but the robo-bull blocked the blow and brought a big yellow gun to bear on the cows. "I am ter-moo-nator T-5," he grated. "Do not move — or you will die."

"Typical ter-moo-nator," McMoo  remarked, holding up his hooves. "Mean, merciless, and no imagination."

Just when Pat thought things couldn't get any scarier, a large brown-and-green buffalo with whopping great horns appeared beside the half-metal monster.

"Well, well," said the buffalo in a silky smooth voice. "So the C.I.A. have built their own flying saucer and found their way to my secret mining base."

"Yep, and it was completely easy-peasy too." Professor McMoo smiled. "You're Toro, I take it — the F.B.I.'s big chief?"

"The very same,"
Toro agreed. "I've been
expecting you for some
time. When I sent Yak
my hungry dinosaur
– and left the plans for a
saucer for him to find –
I knew the fool would send
his three star agents
after me."

"Is that so," said McMoo airily.
"Where did you get that dinosaur, by the
way?"

Toro smiled. "Why, from outer space, of
course."

"Be serious," Bo snapped.

"I am being serious!" Toro insisted. "The
C.I.A. kept beating my plans in the past,
so I searched in the future for ways to
destroy them. And I found out that in the
year 7000 AD, space-exploring humans
in those fabulous flying saucers will make
contact with intelligent, alien dinosaurs."

"Imagine that," breathed McMoo.

Bo had gone cross-eyed. "Dinosaurs in space . . . ? Whoa!"

Pat's brain was boggling. "But why did you kidnap one and bring it back to Earth?"

"To learn its funny dinosaur language, of course!" Toro tapped T-5's ringblender. "Thanks to this, we can understand every growl and roar . . ."

"Let's see if you understand *this*!" Bo snarled. Tearing open her spacesuit, she blasted Toro with a jet of high-pressure milk from her blue-and-green udder! The buffalo reeled backwards – helped along by a hefty kick in the chest from Pat.

At the same time, McMoo shoved T-5 back through the hatch with all his strength. "Run!" he yelled, quickly bundling Bo and Pat away down the corridor.

"Stop!" T-5 fired a jet of scalding, stinking slime after them. "I will disable you with cream-cheese."

"Tempting offer," McMoo yelled back, "but I think we'd rather escape!"

As T-5 chased after the C.I.A. agents, Toro checked a space scanner on his wrist — and smiled. A large egg-shaped spaceship was approaching the Jaggonax Cluster. "Your timing couldn't be better, Professor," he murmured. "More visitors are on their way. I must leave before they arrive." He turned and stalked away to his saucer. "My trap is ready to be sprung . . . and McMoo, Pat and Bo will be its unwitting victims!"

Chapter Six

RACING TO DANGER

Galloping desperately along the space-base corridor, Pat felt his heart racing even faster than his hooves. "I suppose the F.B.I.'s boss was bound to have a tough ter-moo-nator bodyguard . . ."

"With a cream-cheese launcher too. Ouch!" McMoo noted. "Red-hot stinky cheese could *seriously* upset our stomachs."

"It could blow them clean off!" Bo agreed – then skidded to a stop as a heavy door slid down from the ceiling in front of them, blocking the way ahead. "Pants. T-5 or Toro must've closed the door by remote control."

Pat turned, spotted a smaller door in the wall and threw it open. "Quick, let's hide in here!"

The cows ducked inside. McMoo slammed the door behind them and quickly locked it.

A light flickered on, and Bo smiled. "Good choice, Pat."

"Pulsating potatoes!" Pat gasped. There were shelves full of weapons all around them! "Whoever blocked our way and made us come in here really messed up!"

"Didn't they just," mused McMoo. "The F.B.I.'s been making a lot of mistakes lately. And yet, Toro said he was expecting us . . ."

Bo wasn't listening. "Their mess-up, our *bless*-up. Now we can fight our way out of here!" She picked up a big silver rifle. "Cool — a sour-cream shotgun."

"And racks of spare ter-moo-nator armour!" Pat said excitedly.

"I don't approve of guns," said McMoo, picking up a cream pistol. "But at least we can protect ourselves."

"Protect ourselves?" Bo grinned. "We can turn ourselves into a three-cow army with this lot. Let's do it ..."

At that very same moment, the *Sauropod* was fast approaching the Jaggonax Cluster.

"The trail goes a bit funny up ahead, Captain," Arx reported.

60

"It's almost as if *two* flying saucers came here . . ."

"You must be mistaken, Arx. There's only one parked down there." Teggs rose up in his control pit as he spotted the unmistakable spacecraft lying on a large chunk of rock. "See? Beside that old space mining base . . ."

"It's got to be T-5's ship," said Gipsy. "Perhaps we'll find his masters here."

"And who knows how many more dinosaur moo-tants." Arx swallowed hard. "How shall we tackle them, Captain?"

"We'll land the *Sauropod* out of sight," said Teggs. "Then we will march across the asteroid and burst into the base with Alass and her special security squad."

Gipsy forced a brave smile. "Those are some of the toughest ankylosaurs in space. With them on our side, we'll soon take care of those creepy killer cow things."

"Let's hope so," said Teggs. He chewed heroically on a small sapling. "Sprite, take the ship down. Operation Cattle-Crunch is under way!"

Down below in the mining base, unaware of the astrosaurs' impending attack, the Cows In Action were getting ready to confront the F.B.I. forces.

Bo had strapped weapons all over

her body. Pat protected himself with a ter-moo-nator breastplate and a cream pistol in each hand. McMoo wore horn-armour and strapped a barrel of super-chilled muck-and-thistle ice cream to his back, ready to use with the *I-scream* cannon he gripped in both hooves.

"Unlock the door, Bo," the professor said.

"I'm surprised the ter-moo-nator hasn't tried to knock it down," said Pat nervously.

Bo sprang from the storeroom with a kung-moo leap – but the corridor outside was deserted. "Ha! That clanking tin of techno-spam is more like a *chicken* than a bull. He must've been too scared to fight us."

"Hmm." McMoo looked doubtful. "This whole escape is beginning to feel a bit too easy. I have a feeling that Toro and T-5 are up to something . . ."

As stealthily as they could while weighed down with their weapons, the cows crept back down the corridor.

"We'll burst in and surprise them," said McMoo as they reached the enormous hatchway. "One . . . two . . . three . . ."

The Cows In Action kicked open the door and charged into a run-down old control room.

There was no sign of Toro.

Ter-moo-nator T-5 stood glaring at them from the middle of the room, his green eyes aglow. Behind him stood six horrifying monsters with heads as big as sofas and claws like carving knives. Their jaws were crammed with teeth like elephant tusks. Dark eyes burned with hatred.

McMoo froze, and signalled Pat and Bo to do the same.

"Space dinosaurs," Pat whispered in disbelief. "For real!"

Bo raised her gun to fire, but the professor shook his head. "Those things have us outnumbered. I think they're T. rexes – the most savage predators ever."

"Kind of weird-looking ones," Bo retorted.

As Pat's shocked senses took in more details, he realized the monsters had cow-horns curving out of their heads like bony lances. Their hides were scaly like a reptile's but patterned black and white like a cow's. Most gruesome of all, udders hung down from each belly like a bundle of pink balloons.

"Are we seeing things?" he said in a daze.

"Yes," T-5 answered in his grating electronic voice. "You are seeing the first ever dinosaur moo-tants."

Bo gulped. "But . . . how?"

"We've come up against mutant moo-tants mixed up by the F.B.I. before," McMoo reminded her, "but nothing like this." His amazing brain was reeling. "Tell us, T-5 – why come all the way out here just to try and turn space dinosaurs into cows?"

"Toro has many plans . . ." T-5 smiled nastily. "As you will discover."

"Where is he now?" McMoo demanded.

"He has business elsewhere," the ter-moo-nator told them. "And now, there is business I must conclude with you . . ."

Drooling and slavering, the dinosaur moo-tants advanced towards the cows. McMoo, Bo and Pat raised their weapons and braced themselves to fight . . .

But suddenly, the moo-tants stopped, lowered their heads and bowed down before the C.I.A. agents!

"Huh?" Bo frowned. "Why are they acting like they *serve* us?"

Meanwhile, Captain Teggs was leading Iggy, Arx and Gipsy through the corridors of the mining base. Alass the ankylosaur and her six-strong squad thumped along behind.

"The control room should be this way," said Iggy.

A loud growling noise filled the air. Everyone froze.

"The moo-tants must be close," Arx whispered.

"Actually, that was my stomach," said Teggs, blushing. "Sorry – I forgot to grab a snack before we left!"

The astrosaurs continued their advance. Gipsy found she'd lost her appetite as she saw a large hatchway up ahead. "That must be the control room."

"Get ready, everyone." Teggs raised his titanic tail. "We're going in!"

BWAMMMMM!!!

With a single sweeping blow, Teggs smashed down the door and led the charge inside.

Arx took in the scene – and gulped. "Looks like we've found the dinosaur moo-tants' secret base, all right."

"Six of them!" Gipsy's head-crest blazed blue with alarm.

"And there's T-5." Teggs watched as the ter-moo-nator and his monsters bowed down to three cows who were armed to the teeth.

"Those must be his no-good bosses," said Iggy.

"Sorry to crash your little party," Teggs called. "But whatever you're planning, we're here to stop you."

"Negative, astrosaurs," roared the ter-moo-nator. "My three masters have ordered DEATH TO ALL DINOSAURS – starting with *you*."

Green laser flashes zapped from T-5's eyes. Teggs gasped and staggered backwards under the onslaught, falling into Arx and Iggy. At the same time, the moo-tants roared and hissed and stamped towards them.

Bravely, Teggs struggled back up. "Arx, Iggy, Gipsy, Alass," he barked. "*Into battle!*"

Chapter Seven

A CLASH OF LEGENDS!

Professor McMoo, Pat and Bo stared in dismay as the space dinosaurs charged forward to take on T-5 and the moo-tants. The whole control room shook as a ma-hoosive fight kicked off!

"You're outnumbered," McMoo yelled at T-5 as he strode into the midst of the battle. "You can't possibly win!"

"That is the whole idea!" T-5 warbled. "These astrosaurs will think they have caught their criminals . . . while Toro remains free to perfect our plans!"

Growls and roars and blistering butter-jets filled the air, and McMoo quickly bundled Pat and Bo behind a bank of controls for shelter. "So now we know," he muttered. "Toro *tricked* us into entering that store and grabbing a ton of armour and weapons."

Bo groaned. "Of course — so we'd look like T-5's really mean masters!"

Pat nodded gloomily. "When these astrosaur things get us, Toro will be free to do whatever he's planning without them or the C.I.A. on his back."

"That's clever, isn't it?" McMoo was actually smiling. "Oooh, isn't that clever? That Toro's a sly one."

"And we'll all be *squished* ones by the time those scary astrosaurs have finished with us." Bo raised her two butter-bazookas. "Let's hope these things can hold them off . . ."

"Arx! Gipsy!" cried Teggs, grappling with a C. rex in the scaly scrum of rampaging moo-tants. "Get T-5's bosses — if we can catch the ringleaders, the rest of this mob should surrender straight away!"

"On it, Captain!" Gipsy joined Arx, and the two astrosaurs fought their way through the furious throng towards the control panels that shielded the moo-tants' masters.

"No!" cried T-5. "I will defend my leaders to the death!" He raised his cream-cheese launcher, but Arx knocked him aside with a hefty paw. T-5 was sent sprawling — straight into two high-velocity hoof-jabs from Gipsy, which punched out the lasers in his eyes. With an electric warble he fell to the floor.

"Nice work, guys!" Teggs called. But there was no time to celebrate. Three C. rexes were attacking Iggy and Alass, hammering them hard with their horns.

Teggs hurled himself into the fray along with two ankylosaur guards, dragging the dairy-dealing demons away.

Arx, meanwhile, found his way blocked by another C. rex that was spoiling for a fight. While he grappled with the gruesome creature, Gipsy finally managed to reach the bank of controls sheltering Bo, Pat and McMoo.

"*Hiiiiiiii-YAH!*" She leaped over the top – straight into a blast from Bo's butter-bazooka! "Ooof!"

"Think yourself lucky I set it to 'warm and sloppy'," cried Bo, "and not 'white-hot doom'!"

Staggering sideways and hearing only triumphant mooing, Gipsy was blinded by the yellow goop. She lashed out with a hoof and landed a lucky blow to Pat's breastplate. *WHUMP!* She knocked the young bullock to the floor.

"Hey!" McMoo fired his *I-scream* cannon at Gipsy's legs and knocked her hooves from under her with a jet of icy slush. "Sorry about this – but we can't let you stop us going after the real bad guys . . . "

Gipsy fell to the floor with a splash and a cry. Bo grabbed the hadrosaur by her armoured tail and swung her around three times before letting go. *Whizzz!* Gipsy went surfing on dairy slush, crashing into the crowd.

"Leave my friend alone!" shouted Arx – or, as the cows heard: "*RRROAAARRRR!*" He lowered his huge head-frill and charged at McMoo. The professor sprayed more muck–

and-thistle ice cream at the oncoming
astrosaur, but Arx jumped over the
puddle – and McMoo couldn't get clear
in time . . .

SPLANGGG!
"Arrrgh!" The professor
was butted into the air –
and with a *CRUNNCH*
his armoured horns
got stuck in the
ceiling! He was left
dangling helplessly,
rubbing his bruised
bottom. "Well, this is
embarrassing!"

"Hang on, Prof!" Bo
called. "I'll get you!"

While Pat drove Arx away
with his pair of splurging cream pistols,
Bo jumped onto the back of a nearby C.
rex, climbed up onto its head and leaped
towards McMoo. She just managed to
grab hold of his hooves.

"Look out, Bo!" McMoo yelled.
"You're pulling my horns out of the
ceiling. We're going to—"

"*FALLLL!*" Bo concluded as they both
went tumbling through the air . . .

Only to land
on Teggs!
While Iggy
and Alass
dealt with
the last
C. rex
standing,
Teggs had
galloped over
to help Gipsy
and Arx. Now he gasped, knocked to
his knees as two sets of hard hooves
crunched against his backplates, and
Bo and McMoo rolled off him onto the
floor.

"A sneaky attack from above, huh?"
Teggs growled. "You'll regret that!"

McMoo saw a stegosaurus tail hurtling towards him and Little Bo like a spiky club. He rolled over to protect the dazed milk-cow – and the tank of hideous ice cream on his back caught the brunt of the bash. *FWOOM!* It exploded, coating him and Bo in the disgusting stuff from head to toe, stunning them both.

"Bo! Professor!" Pat ran over and started to haul them towards the exit.

But now Teggs had recovered. Sweaty, scratched and battle-weary, he and Iggy blocked the C.I.A. agents' escape – while a soaked and slippery Arx and Gipsy closed in from behind.

"One final try," said Little Bo bravely. She let Teggs and Iggy have a big blast of butter, and followed it up with super-squirts of cold milk from her udder. "Prof, Pat – run for it!"

As Iggy bent over, wiping his eyes, Pat leapfrogged the iguanodon – but landed badly in a puddle of steaming cream cheese. He slipped and banged his head. "Oww!"

Iggy sat on him. "Now you're down, son, just stay there!"

"Little bruv!" Bo dived forward and skidded through Teggs's legs on her belly, trying to reach Pat. But Teggs thumped his tail down on her back and stopped her slide, pinning her to the floor. "Hey! Let go!" she mooed crossly.

Professor McMoo knew there was no
chance of escape now. He held up his
hooves in what he hoped was a universal
sign of surrender. Gipsy and Arx took an
arm each in a firm grip.

"I wish I could make you understand,"
said McMoo sadly. "We're really the
good guys of the cattle world!"

"I've heard enough mooing for one
day," said Teggs. "Let's take them all to the
Sauropod – and lock them in the cells!"

Thousands of miles away, in a dark
and secret lair on the fringes of the
Carnivore Sector, Toro sat in sinister
silence with a massive meat-eating
dinosaur and several big-toothed guards.
Using long-range spy-scopes, they were
secretly listening in on the *Sauropod's*
communications.

"*It's good news, Admiral Rosso!*"
came Teggs's voice at last, weary but
triumphant. "*We've captured T-5, the*

dinosaur moo-tants and their masters, and used space magnets to pull their flying saucer on board. Whoever they are, they can't cause us any more trouble now . . ."

The meat-eater laughed. "You are sssso wrong, Captain! You believe you have won – and yet you have no idea of the real danger . . ."

"I told you my plan would work perfectly," said Toro smugly. "We have tested out our creations on the most powerful plant-eaters around. We have studied their strengths and weaknesses. Now we can create new, improved dinosaur moo-tants – ready for phase two of our grand scheme . . ."

"Enjoy your victory while you can, plant-eaters . . ." The meat-eater bared his deadly teeth in a smile. "Ssssoon, the Jurassic Quadrant will belong to carnivores alone . . . and then old Mother Earth will feel our bite!"

Chapter Eight

COM-MOO-NICATION TROUBLE

"Well, this isn't exactly an ideal situation, is it?" called Professor McMoo from his cell on board the *Sauropod*. He was sharing it with a sleeping C. rex. Pat and Bo were locked up to his left, and he sighed at them through the bars. "They haven't even brought us a cup of tea."

"Never mind, Prof," said Bo. "We've been in worse scrapes than this."

"Have we?" Pat sighed too. "We're a gazillion miles from home, with no way back; we're the prisoners of space dinosaurs who don't speak our language and think we're evil *and* we smell like a sewage pipe in the devil's own dairy."

"Right now, the language barrier is our biggest problem . . ." Suddenly, McMoo sat up so fast his specs almost flew off. "Of course! T-5 can speak the local lingo. Toro kidnapped that torvosaurus we met back in Luckyburger to learn its language, and programmed the results into T-5's ringblender . . ."

Pat nodded with excitement. "If we could only get hold of that, we could use it to tell these astrosaurs who their real enemy is!"

"But how can we get out?" Bo heaved on the bars helplessly.

"I still have my trusty screwdriver." McMoo pulled the simple tool out of the sleeve of his spacesuit and jammed it into the lock. "You know, I was thinking of adding a vibration circuit to this thing, so it produced ultrasonic sound waves . . ."

"A sonic screwdriver?" Bo snorted. "Who would ever use one of those?"

Just then, the cell door clicked open. "Aha! The screwdriver worked the old-fashioned way." McMoo waggled his eyebrows at his young friends. "Now, I must find T-5 and get that ringblender. I'll be back as soon as I can!"

In the astrosaurs' crew room, Teggs, Arx, Iggy and Gipsy were relaxing after their battle.

"I'm glad we've got those horrible cow things under control," said Gipsy, sniffing herself cautiously. "I had to take fifteen showers to wash away the stink of that yukky dairy stuff."

"I had to have twenty-five," said Iggy. "You wouldn't believe where I found lumps of cream-cheese—"

Arx pulled a face. "Please, don't tell us!"

"Something's puzzling me," Teggs announced, crunching hungrily on his hundredth coconut.

"How come the metal cow could talk our language, but his masters couldn't?"

"Maybe T-5's robot brain contains a language computer?" said Gipsy.

"He's probably got all sorts of nasty talents," Iggy agreed. "Like those lasers he had in his eyes."

"That's another thing," said Teggs. "Those three cows had loads of weapons. They could've really hurt or even killed us – but they chose not to, and surrendered."

"Perhaps that's why they turn regular dinos into cow-monsters," said Iggy. "They don't have the bottle for fighting, so they get others to do their dirty work for them."

"Perhaps," Teggs agreed. "But there was something about them. They looked . . . kind. Clever."

"Not too clever now, are they?" said Iggy breezily. "Locked up in our cells."

"*Alert!*" squawked the alarm pterosaur, her voice echoing through the ship. "*Cell open! Prisoner loose on level six! Look out, all! SQUAAWWWWK!*"

The astrosaurs jumped to their feet. Gipsy looked at Iggy. "What was that you were saying, Ig?"

"Say it again on the way down to the cells," said Teggs, scoffing a few more coconuts to keep his strength up. "It looks like the battle's not over yet!"

As the alarm went off, Professor McMoo quickened his step, hunting for the banged-up ter-moo-nator. At last he found T-5 on his own, slumped in the cell on the end.

The screwdriver made short work of the lock. McMoo opened the door and hurried inside, knowing he could be recaptured at any moment. He grabbed the ringblender and pulled . . .

But it was stuck tight in the ter-moo-nator's robotic snout.

McMoo studied it more closely.

T-5 had clearly been whacked in the face — the ringblender would not come free. Frantically, McMoo set to work with the screwdriver once again.

Then a roar behind him made him realize that his time had run out ...

He turned to find the stegosaurus and his friends standing outside the cell – and they did not look happy!

"What are you doing, cow?" Teggs demanded, standing in the doorway. "Wasn't your own cell comfy enough?"

"Looks like he was trying to wake up his robot servant," said Gipsy.

Iggy nodded. "Well, at least it saves us the effort of locking him up again ..."

Finally, with a snort of effort, McMoo pulled the robot's metal nose clean off!

"Ouch!" Arx frowned. "I'm not sure you wanted to do that."

"Oh yes, I bottom did!" said the professor suddenly, wearing the robo-conk over his own with the ring dangling down. "This botty device was translating the ter-moo-nator's buns language into bum-bum dino-speak, and it'll do the same for me!"

The astrosaurs turned to each other in surprise.

"He's talking our language!" said Teggs. "What's with all that bottom stuff, though?"

"My friends and I aren't bad wobbly-cheeks!" McMoo went on. "I'm Professor Angus McMoo, a booty agent for the time-travelling cattle investigation squad, the butt Cows In Action."

Gipsy's head-crest blushed purple. "Why do you keep talking about bottoms?"

"I don't mean to!" McMoo banged the ring with his hoof. "This buns-of-steel thing must have got damaged in the fight. The *real* bad guy who programmed it learned your bum-bum language from a torvosaurus."

"Ah, that explains it," said Iggy, nodding knowingly. "Those torvosaurus types are always going on about bums."

"Their motto is: *The bigger your rear, the*

more there is to fear," Teggs agreed. "But tell me, 'Professor' – why should we believe you? You *would* say that this is someone else's fault, to save your own hide."

"Captain Teggs is right," said Arx. "We followed the light-atom trail of your flying saucer to Jaggonax – and, sure enough, there it was."

"The botty saucer you followed belongs to shake-your-tush Toro, the Buffalo-in-Chief of the Fed-up Bull Institute," McMoo insisted. "We followed his bummy-bummy trail to Jaggonax too – Toro must've boosted his saucer's backside photon drive on purpose to lure us all there – so you would find us bottom and think we big-buns were to blame for rump wobble-bot attacking you."

Teggs turned uncertainly to Arx. "Is that possible?"

"With fewer bottoms, it's *distinctly* possible," Arx confirmed.

"I'm in charge of communications," said Gipsy. "I'm sure I can fix this fault in the translator." She walked up to McMoo, plucked off the false nose and studied the ringblender. "Give me your astro-tweezers, Ig . . ."

Iggy passed her the tool. Gipsy opened up part of the scorched silver ring and quickly got to work. "There!" She handed it back to McMoo. "That should fix it."

"Astounding!" McMoo studied her handiwork. "And to think dinosaurs have a reputation for being stupid on planet Earth . . ."

"Excuse me?" said Teggs sternly.

"Nobody believes you had the technology needed to leave the planet," McMoo explained. "Well, except for this one crazy author, but no one ever listens to him . . ." He beamed. "Isn't it marvellous to have met like this? Think of what we can learn from each other. The knowledge we can share! The wisdom! The tea bags!"

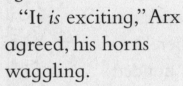

"It *is* exciting," Arx agreed, his horns waggling.

"Before we share anything with you cows," said Iggy, "how do we know we can really trust you?"

"Hmm. Good question. Luckily, I have a good answer." McMoo pulled out his screwdriver and fiddled with the ringblender's exposed insides. "If I can just boost this ringblender's range so it will translate any cattle in the area . . ."

T–5 stirred with an electronic warble.

"Quickly," McMoo hissed, shoving T–5's snout back into its proper place, but keeping the nose-ring himself. "Lock me in and get out of sight – but stay where you can hear!"

Teggs hesitated. "What are you up to?"

"You'll soon see." McMoo looked at him with pleading eyes. "Please, Captain Teggs?"

"All right, Professor," Teggs said at last.

The astrosaurs left the cell, shut the door and retreated round the corner as T–5 sat up.

"You beef-brained nit!" McMoo scowled at the ter-moo-nator. "You've got us *all* locked up on the astrosaurs' ship."

"Excellent," said T–5, not realizing his nose-ring was missing. "All goes according to Toro's plans. We take the blame, while he works on in safety."

"Yep, you've tricked the astrosaurs into thinking we Cows In Action are

95

to blame," McMoo went on. "The only good news is that the astrosaurs will lock *you* up as well as us."

"Not for long," T-5 grated. "Once the Vegetarian Sector has been invaded by new moo-tants, Toro will set me free to lead a killer-carnivore attack on the people of Earth – while you will be left here to rot . . ."

"An attack on outer space *and* the Earth?" McMoo felt sick. "The F.B.I. are really thinking big this time . . ."

Just then, Teggs burst back into the cell. "All right, we've heard enough. Out you come, Professor."

McMoo beamed. "Thought you'd never ask, Captain!"

"Noooooo!" The ter-moo-nator scowled helplessly at the professor. "You have tricked me!"

"Yep – and it's as plain as the nose on your face." McMoo tugged off T-5's hooter. Then he and Teggs jumped out of the cell and locked the door.

"I'm sorry we attacked you and your friends, McMoo," said Iggy.

"It's clear that this Toro is the real enemy," Gipsy added.

"Right," said Arx. "And from this moment, we'll all work together to stop him."

"Astrosaurs teaming up with Cows In Action? What a fabulous idea!" McMoo threw an arm around Teggs's neck. "Now, let's get on with finding the real bad guys. There's a double invasion on the cards – and we're running out of time to stop it!"

Chapter Nine

FIGHTING BACK

Pat and Bo were both jubilant and *moo*bilant when the professor came along with Teggs to set them free. Iggy led all three C.I.A. agents to the bathroom, where they washed down their stinky spacesuits and cleaned up in the *Sauropod*'s ENORMOUS showers.

Gipsy and Iggy, meanwhile, copied T–5's translator-ring and built two more for Pat and Bo to wear.

Once they were in place, everyone could understand each other. To seal their new alliance, Teggs and his crew took the C.I.A. agents to the ship's canteen to feast on plants and grasses, washed down with a trough of swamp tea.

"It's out of this world," McMoo declared, swigging back the steaming drink. "Tea brewed from a sludgy alien swamp! Imagine that! *Taste* that!"

Bo and Pat did so. They were almost sick on the spot.

"I think I'll stick to water," Pat managed politely.

"I'll stick to milk!" Bo rinsed her mouth out with a few squirts from her  udder, gargled and gulped. "Ahh, that's the stuff! And there's plenty for all of you!" She squirted some more milk into four cups. "Who's first?"

Teggs, Arx and Gipsy took nervous sips
– but Iggy knocked back his glass in one
go. "Ahhh! Cool and creamy."

Bo winked. "Just like me!"

The new friends chatted about
everything from the sunset on Corytho
to the price of tea bags in twenty-first-
century supermarkets . . . from the last
days of the dinosaurs on Earth to the
time-travelling escapades of Clever
Cows . . . from Professor McMoo's many
inventions to Teggs's many ten-course
breakfasts.

But once the food and drink was finished, it was time to get down to business in the *Sauropod*'s meeting room.

"Things to do," Teggs announced. "We need to track down Toro in the Carnivore Sector . . . discover his invasion plans—"

"And then stop him," Bo chipped in. "Ideally by punching his lights out."

Iggy smiled. "I like your style, Little Bo!"

Bo batted her eyelashes. "I quite like your cap, Jiggy. But it would be better if you cut it up, painted it pink and stuck a feather in the top."

"Jiggy?" Gipsy winked at him. "Now that really *is* style!"

"Cap makeovers aside, it's still quite a to-do list, isn't it?" said Arx.

"What worries me is, how did Toro get hold of so many T. rexes to turn into C. rexes?" McMoo frowned, deep in thought. "And if he's planning invasions both here and back on Earth, he must have an awful lot more . . ."

"You think someone is supplying Toro with deadly dinos to turn into moo-tants?" said Teggs.

"An ally in the Carnivore Sector," breathed Arx.

Pat gulped. "Toro framed the three of us to keep the astrosaurs *and* the C.I.A. off his back, to buy himself more time . . ."

"Time to build an invasion force of new dino moo-tants!" said Bo.

"On Planet Sixty, T-5 seemed to be testing that C. rex," Teggs muttered. "Testing it for weaknesses, perhaps."

"Weaknesses that Toro can remove from a second batch?" Gipsy shuddered. "I didn't notice many myself."

"We must take a closer look," Arx

declared. "We must study those moo-tants and see how they were made."

"Then perhaps you and the prof can work out how to deal with them," Iggy added.

"Definitely!" boomed McMoo. "I suspect that Arx is very nearly as clever as I am."

"Thank you, Professor," said Arx drily. "Perhaps Pat could be our assistant? He seems to have a good head on his shoulders."

Pat nodded super-quickly, as if to prove it.

"Good plan," said Teggs. "Meantime, how do we find Toro? This time, he's covered his tracks. There's a path leading from Jaggonax into the Carnivore Sector . . . but from there, it's too faint to follow."

"The moo-tants are made from T. rexes," Iggy pointed out. "Maybe Toro's hiding out near Teerex Major?"

"Is that a planet? A whole planet of T. rexes?" McMoo marvelled. "This Jurassic Quadrant of yours sounds incredible!"

"Can we fly there and ask if anyone's seen Toro?" asked Pat.

"Only if you want your answer in missiles and laser beams," said Gipsy. "Plant-eater dinos aren't allowed in carnivore space. Evil alien bulls might get in — but velociraptor death ships would zap us as soon as we enter."

"What about that ter-moo-nator thing?" said Arx. "T-5 serves Toro — he might know where he is."

"You'll never make a ter-moo-nator talk," said McMoo. "He'll lock down his computer brain."

"I'm pretty good with robots," said Iggy, standing up. "I'll give it a go."

"Those techno beef-heads can get pretty nasty." Bo linked arms with the iguanodon. "I'll go with you, Jiggy — and be your *Bo*-dyguard!"

"Er . . . great,"
said Iggy,
blushing.

"Arx, you
and the
professor had
better get to
work too," said
Teggs.

"Yep! Lead on, big fella!" McMoo and
Pat followed Arx from the room, and
Iggy and Bo left after them.

"What about us, Captain?" said Gipsy.

"In some ways, we have the hardest
job," said Teggs. "We must think of a way
to get into meat-eater space without
starting a war – before Toro and his
friends start their own!"

The cows and the astrosaurs got straight
to work.

Arx, the professor and Pat bundled a
C. rex into the *Sauropod*'s medical lab.

"We can put him through a super-cell scanner," Arx suggested. "It will tell us how much of him has turned cow and how much is still T. rex."

"Great!" said McMoo. "Let's check the DNA-flux too – that will tell us whether the change is reversible or if he's stuck this way for ever."

"Good thinking!" said Arx with excitement. "Of course, if we add in an impact-sweeper to the scanner, we can find out what changed this T. rex – a chemical injection, or a molecule ray—"

"Or we could try asking him!" said Pat brightly as the moo-tant's eyes flicked open. "Excuse me, Mr C. rex, have you any idea what turned you into a moo-tant?"

The cow-dino considered. "Er . . . me seem to recall it was gas. Yellow gas. It smelled like scummy old pond."

"I see," said Pat. "And where did you meet Toro?"

"On Jaggonax," the C. rex went on.
"Me and my pals is miners. Us meant
to meet torvosaurus ambassador there
– want to buy asteroids for drilling. But
then dumb buffalo and metal thing show
up and gas us."

"So *that's* how Toro got his C. rexes."
Arx blinked. "Who'd have thought a
cow-dino would be so helpful?"

"Let's not
knock it," murmured McMoo.

"Thank you," Pat told the C. rex.
"We're going to try and turn you back
to normal."

"Good," said the patient. "Buffalo said future cows might just undo what  he done, but stinky plant-eating dinos stood no chance …"

Arx raised his eyebrows. "We'll see about that!"

"Now, me knock myself out so you can begin experiments." So saying, the C. rex conked himself on the head and started snoring.

"You heard him, Arx," said McMoo, winking at Pat. "Let's begin!"

Meanwhile, Iggy and Bo were visiting T-5 in his cell.

"We want to know who Toro is working with," said Iggy, "and where they are right now."

"I will tell you nothing," said T-5.

"Oh, yeah?" From behind his back,

Iggy pulled out something that looked like a large gun.

"I do not fear your weapon," T-5 sneered.

"You should fear *these* weapons." Bo held out her hooves. "You're only *part-robot*, after all. And the bits that are still beef I'm going to ... TICKLE!"

Suddenly, she pounced on him like a tickle-ninja. Her hooves dug into his ribs, nudged at his knees and jiggled in his armpits.

"Nooooo!" warbled the robo-bull, bucking and wriggling and giggling under Bo's expert assault. "Ha-ha-ha! Tickling does not compute! Ha-ha— noooo ..."

While T–5 was laughing helplessly, Iggy stepped quickly into the cell and placed his funny-looking gun against the top of the ter-moo-nator's head. *ZUMMMMMM!* Instead of a ray coming out, a blur of light rose up from T–5's head and into the device!

"Hey!" said T–5 as Bo quickly jumped clear. "What did you do?"

Iggy patted his "gun" proudly. "This is an info-sucker — extracts information from computers. I now have a copy of all the data-files in your metal head."

"But if I hadn't distracted you with that tickle attack, you'd have resisted," said Bo. "Or you might have tried to make something up."

"Now we can simply download your data into our own computers and search out all the juicy bits." Iggy gave him a cheery wave as he and Bo left the cell. "Thanks!"

"That's not fair!" T–5 groaned. "You

tricked me."

"Actually, I think you'll find we *TRICKLED* you . . ." Bo blew a gum bubble. "So long, beef-brain!"

Back on the *Sauropod's* flight deck, Gipsy was overseeing the dimorphodon in an extraordinary task. Holding needles in their delicate claws  and beaks, the little flying reptiles sewed dark scales onto a large saggy sack.  Sprite was sticking on two amber jewels that looked almost like eyes . . .

Teggs walked in. "How's the disguise coming along, Gipsy?"

"I wish we had more time," she sighed. "Have you told Admiral Rosso what we're doing?"

"I can't," he said sadly. "If carnivores overheard, it would spoil our whole plan."

"But couldn't he send more ships to help us?" asked Gipsy.

"No way." Teggs shook his head. "The meat-eaters would never believe that we were looking for a criminal. They'd think we were trying to invade."

"I suppose you're right." Gipsy looked at the black-and-green costume and nodded. "All right, everyone. I think the captain's ready for his new look."

The dimorphodon flapped into the air and dropped the dark sack over Teggs's head, neck and upper body. It was a home-made carnivore fancy-dress costume.

"Hmm, not bad," said Gipsy. "As long as no one looks too closely . . ."

Suddenly, the doors swished open, and Iggy walked in with Bo. "Captain, we've copied T-5's computer brain. Now we just need to search his memory files to find where Toro's gone—" He broke off and jumped in the air with shock. "Whoa! It's a torvosaurus!"

"Just like that one I saw in the twenty-sixth century." Bo scowled. "Quick – clobber it!"

"No need!" Teggs poked his head through the outfit's mouth-hole. "It's only me!"

Gipsy gave Sprite and the dimorphodon a thumbs-up. "Nice work, guys – we fooled them!"

"Sorry to shock you," Teggs went on. "We copied the costume from pictures of the *real* missing ambassador."

"But why the dressing-up bit, Teggsy?" asked Bo. "What's the plan?"

"You'll soon see," said Teggs gravely. "But if I mess things up, the *Sauropod* will be destroyed and we will all be killed."

Iggy shrugged. "If you don't try, the whole Vegetarian Sector could be doomed."

Bo gulped. "And Earth as I know it too."

"So there's no choice." Teggs crossed to Gipsy's station and spoke to the whole ship. "Attention, all crew, this is your captain. We are about to embark on the most dangerous mission of our lives. Stand by for action – Carnivore Sector, here we come!"

Chapter Ten

BORDER TO DANGER

Within half an hour, the *Sauropod* had entered the fringes of the Carnivore Sector.

Teggs eyed the scanner nervously. He knew that the fierce and fearsome Raptor Border Patrol would be streaking towards them even now. Arx, Pat and Professor McMoo were still studying the C. rex. Iggy and Bo were sitting in front of computer screens, trawling through the contents of T-5's head, desperately hunting for the vital clue they needed to track down Toro and his allies . . .

"Captain," said Gipsy urgently. "We've been spotted. We're receiving a message –

from a raptor death ship."

Teggs saw it on the scanner – a sharp, pointed spacecraft with a blood-red tip, flying straight for them like an evil arrow.

"With a torvosaurus in the *Sauropod*'s driving seat, we might just survive," he muttered, struggling into the carnivore costume. "Gipsy, let's hear what they have to say."

"*Attention, plant-eaters.*" The cold voice hissed through the speakers. "*Thisss is the Raptor Border Patrol. You have entered carnivore ssspace without permission. Prepare to be killed!*"

"At least they get to the point," said Bo.

"Put them on the screen, Gipsy," Teggs cried, his heart thumping. "Let's hope their eyesight's not perfect!"

The image of two orange raptors in green caps and uniforms appeared on the scanner.

"Don't shoot!" Teggs said in a deep, gruff voice. "I am a carnivore like you. And I have a big butt. A very big butt indeed. Yes."

A tense silence ensued.

One of the raptors narrowed his eyes. "Who are you?"

"I am the torvosaurus ambassador who was kidnapped . . ." Teggs turned to Gipsy, who was out of view of the border patrol, and hissed: "What's my name again?"

"Cindy," Gipsy hissed back.

"Cindy! That's my name," said Teggs, sweat pouring off him inside the costume. "I'm huge, whopping-butt Cindy. Some puny, skinny-bottomed plant-eaters attacked me and took me away – but I stole one of their ships and escaped."

"Ha! Well done," hissed the second guard.

"But what did they do to you?" asked his friend. "You look rubbish."

"So would you if you'd lived on moss and grass for weeks," Teggs said, even more gruffly. "I'm on my way back to Torvox so I can complain to the huge-cheeked High One and get her to attack those rubbish, tiny-bunned leaf-nibblers!"

"Good work," said the first guard. "All right, you can passss."

"But we'll be checking up on your ssstory," said the second.

Teggs gulped. "Um . . ."

"BUTT we'll be checking – get it?"

The raptor winked. "It's a bottom joke! Ha! Have a nice day!"

"Oh, yeah." Teggs tried to chuckle. "Sssee you!"

Gipsy ended the call, and the dimorphodon helped Teggs out of his dripping wet costume. "Well done, Captain!" she said proudly.

"Let's get out of here," said Teggs. "Iggy, Bo – any idea of what direction yet?"

"Yes!" Iggy jumped up excitedly. "According to T-5, Toro is hiding out on Muckspit Point, the only dry land on Bloodsnarl Two."

Bo peered over his shoulder. "Apparently, your meat-eater mates just had a big conference there."

"The League of Galactic Carnivores," Gipsy realized. "What a perfect opportunity for Toro to buddy up with mean dinosaurs."

"But who?" Teggs wondered. "Well, let's go full speed ahead for Bloodsnarl Two. Luckily, we won't pass too close to any carnivore worlds on the way . . ."

Iggy ran to Arx's controls and checked some dials. "Engines stoked to maximum." A hum of power began to build as the *Sauropod* picked up speed, and he smiled over at Bo. "My team have just added some cowpats to the usual dung, so we'll see how they burn . . ."

Suddenly –
WHOOOOOOOOOOSH!
The ship shot forward like a firework. The dimorphodon flapped about in excitement and Teggs, Gipsy and Iggy clung on for dear life.

"Woo-hoo-moooooo!" cried Bo, holding onto a computer. "I guess cowpats burn very, *very* well!"

"At this
rate we'll make
the journey in under
an hour!" cried Gipsy.

Teggs pressed a button on his
communicator. "Arx, any news on
sorting out the moo-tants?"

"We're still trying to return them
to normal," Arx reported. "Nothing's
worked so far, and I'm afraid that sudden
jolt made us spill our latest chemical
mix . . ."

"All over me," came a groan from Pat.

"Whoops! Sorry," said Teggs. "Listen,

guys, we think Toro is on the planet Bloodsnarl Two. But I don't know how long we have before carnivores spot us."

"Toro must've made the journey to and from the Vegmeat Zone in his flying saucer," said McMoo. "Perhaps a small group could scout around in *our* saucer while the *Sauropod* hides somewhere close by – ready to move in when we give the signal?"

"That's a great idea," said Teggs. "I'll have your saucer brought into the shuttle bay. Gipsy, you and I will go."

"I must come too," McMoo's voice insisted. "Toro is the C.I.A.'s responsibility. Pat can stay and help Arx with his cow-dino experiments—"

"Once I've had a shower," Pat chipped in.

"And I'll go as well to look after the prof," said Bo firmly.

"All right," said Teggs. "Iggy, I'm leaving you in charge of the *Sauropod*.

Look after her, old friend – and the crew."

Iggy saluted. "I understand, Captain. Just . . . watch yourselves, OK?"

"Now, before things get too soppy up here, let's go!" Bo blew Iggy a kiss and threw an arm around Gipsy's tail. "Come on, sister. It's time for action!"

Pat hurried through the *Sauropod*'s enormous corridors, ready to shower away the yukky chemicals that had spilled all over him. He felt troubled. The C. rex had said that Arx and his kind couldn't undo the moo-tant effect, and that only future cows might stand a chance. Perhaps that was why the usually brilliant professor (from the present day) and the clearly super-clever triceratops had failed to turn the moo-tant back to normal.

As he entered the bathroom, Pat was hit by a horrid smell. Then he saw the C.I.A. spacesuits hanging up to dry. "That's funny – we washed them. They shouldn't still be smelly . . ."

The stink was coming from inside McMoo's spacesuit. Pat reached inside . . .

. . . and gasped as he pulled out a bunch of soggy wet herbal tea bags from the twenty-sixth century!

Suddenly, Pat remembered the C. rex's description of the gas responsible for its moo-tation – "It smelled like scummy old pond."

And then he remembered Bo holding her nose when the professor was given his tea outside the Palace of Great Moos.

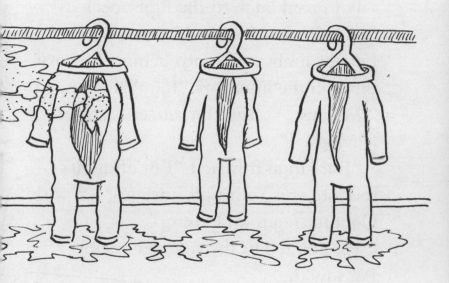

"That stuff stinks like a dredged pond!" she'd said.

"Maybe that amazing Amazon herb in the tea bags is the missing ingredient?

The ox said it had special medicinal properties . . . and only a future cow would know about it!" Pat felt excitement flutter in his tum. "Good job Yak gave the professor a whole box of tea bags we can experiment with . . ." He groaned. "Oh, no. They're on board . . . the C.I.A. saucer!"

Pat raced back to the flight deck as fast as his hooves would carry him. Finally, limbs and lungs aching, he burst through the lift doors. "Iggy!" he gasped. "We must . . . stop the saucer . . . from leaving . . ."

"Eh?" Iggy frowned. "I'm afraid it's too late, son. Your pals have just left with Captain Teggs and Gipsy."

He pointed to the scanner screen. Pat saw the saucer already whizzing away into the starry blackness.

Chapter Eleven

UNDERGROUND FACE-OFF!

"What's going on, Pat?" asked Iggy, leading the young bullock to Gipsy's chair so he could catch his breath.

"We must . . . call them . . . back," Pat panted.

"Sorry, no chance. The carnivores might overhear our message." Iggy frowned. "What's so important?"

"Tea!" Pat wailed, holding up the soggy, stinky bag. "I have to talk to Arx . . . I might be wrong and this might be nothing . . . or it might just prove to be the most important tea bag in history!"

★

In the super-speedy saucer, it took just minutes to reach Bloodsnarl Two. McMoo, Teggs, Gipsy and Bo stared out at its crimson oceans as they sped over the horizon.

"Look!" McMoo pointed to a distant jagged island. "That must be Muckspit Point . . ."

"And look what's parked outside," said Teggs. "The F.B.I. saucer – and a whopping great space transporter!"

"I've never seen one that big before," said Gipsy, her head-crest glowing blue. "If only Iggy were here, he'd recognize the design."

"Well, it's a carnivore ship, for certain," said Teggs. When Bo and McMoo looked puzzled, he pointed. "You can tell by the crimson skull painted on the side."

"Nice," said Bo. "Well, whoever they are, the sooner we biff them up, the better."

"We'd better head back to the *Sauropod*

and organize a full-on assault force," Teggs agreed. "This could get messy."

But suddenly the saucer came to a jolting halt in mid-air.

"It very nearly *did* get messy," McMoo gasped. "If it wasn't for the gravity straps, we'd be splatted all over the walls!"

Gipsy stared helplessly at the controls. "Have we hit something?"

"No." Teggs looked at the yellow light that had engulfed the window. "We've been caught by a magnetic ray – and it's dragging us down to Muckspit Point!"

"Pants!" cried Bo. "We've been spotted."

"I know we're not supposed to contact the *Sauropod*," said Gipsy, "but this is an emergency . . ."

"It's no good." McMoo could see the control dials waving and flicking about. "The magnetic field is blocking our communications."

The saucer was forced down with a crunch and the celestial sat-nav spoke up calmly: "*You have been forced down onto a remote planet.*" A heavy metallic  thumping started up. "*And now unidentified life-forms with big teeth are breaking down the door so they can come in and get you.*"

"Yeah – not actually helping much, thanks," the professor told it.

As the gravity straps were released, Teggs looked at the others. "I think we'd better open the doors. If we don't, the saucer will be smashed and we'll never be able to use it to escape."

"Optimistic and practical, Captain. You make sense." McMoo took a deep breath and pressed the door button. "Brace yourselves, everyone . . . here comes company!"

The outer doors slid open, and six C. rexes stomped inside, horns gleaming, udders wobbling. McMoo and Gipsy tried to fight them off, and Teggs and Bo even landed a couple of blows — but it was no good. Their attackers were too

massive, leaving little room to move. Grunting, growling and mooing, the C. rexes grabbed the saucer's occupants and hauled them outside.

Helpless in the scaly grip of his captor, McMoo caught a glimpse of the vast scarlet sea splashing hard against the rocks. Then, together with Teggs, Bo and Gipsy, he was forced inside a tunnel. It wound down and around into darkness . . .

Finally, the cows and astrosaurs were shoved into a vast arena, surrounded by row upon row of stone thrones and benches. The C. rexes stood guard behind them.

Gipsy looked around in awe. "So this is where the League of Galactic Carnivores hold their yearly meetings."

"It's a fleapit," said Bo. "They should install some disco lights and a pumping sound system."

"I'd sooner they added a dozen or so emergency exits," said McMoo.

A strong, familiar smell spread through the air.

"What a whiff!" Teggs spluttered. "It's worse than a mammoth's armpits."

Gipsy covered her nose. "I've never smelled anything like it before."

"I have," said Bo. "It's like that horrible twenty-sixth-century tea you were swilling, Professor!"

"Plurge!" McMoo agreed, licking his lips. "Yes, of course. Made with a special herb from the Amazon rainforest in Toro's time, remember?"

"*And that herb is the key to our power!*"

Teggs, Gipsy, Bo and McMoo turned at the sound of the harsh, bragging voice.

There, posing on the steps of the rocky
stadium in front of a mini control room,
stood Toro, in all his big-horned buffalo
glory.

But it was not Toro who had spoken.
Standing beside him was a grisly sight:
a bloated grey velociraptor with yellow
eyes and rows of pointed teeth to match.
He wore a blood-stained cloak with
fangs sewn into the hem, and a crown
carved from dinosaur bones.

"I don't believe
it," breathed Gipsy.
"That's . . . that's . . ."

"The Raptor
Royal." Teggs put
his tail around Gipsy
protectively. "Warrior
King of Raptos.
The strongest,
most bloodthirsty
carnivore ruler in
space!"

"A velociraptor," McMoo mused.
"Hmmm. I'm guessing they haven't
evolved into sweet, lovely creatures with
a passion for pressing wild flowers?"

Teggs shook his head. "They're one of
the cruellest, cleverest carnivore races of
all. They've started dozens of wars and
conquered untold planets."

Bo shivered. "If these raptor scumbags
are helping Toro, no wonder he wasn't
bothered by their border patrol."

"Greetings, astrosaurs," wheezed the

revolting raptor. "Welcome, cattle. You were fools to think you could ssssurprise us." He waved a claw at the control centre behind him. "I built thisss place myself. Its early warning ssssystem detected your approach – and its ssssspace magnet drew you down here."

McMoo beamed. "Just in time for a friendly chat!"

"Of course." The Raptor Royal grinned grotesquely. "I like to get to know my food before I eat it."

Bo snorted. "I can tell you now, ugly — we're not going to get on!"

"Just tell us one thing, your revoltingness," said Teggs. "Why in space are you helping that buffalo beside you, instead of eating him?"

"He has given me the means to destroy the likes of *you*," rasped the raptor.

"Indeed I have," said Toro smugly.

"And we can see you're dying to tell us about it," said Gipsy. "So — how is some whiffy tea going to give you anything besides bad breath?"

"That special herb is the key ingredient in my moo-tant transformation," said Toro. "When boiled together with special chemicals, it gives me swift and precise powers to transform bodies and minds to whatever purpose I decide . . ."

"Boiled?" McMoo frowned in concentration. "Then that yellow gas one of your C. rexes told us about was actually yellow *steam* . . ."

"Yes, blabbing too much was one of the things we had to fix in the mark-one dinosaur moo-tants," Toro admitted. "As time passes, they grow far too kind and gentle – too much like normal cows."

"Yes, us do!" piped up one of the C. rexes standing guard behind them. "Sorry, your bull-ness."

"Ssssilence, dolt!" roared the Raptor Royal. The C. rex cringed and fell silent.

Toro glared at Teggs and Gipsy. "T-5 lured you to Planet Sixty to test a moo-tant in combat against you. That battle revealed other things that required improvement."

Teggs remembered, "The C. rex was a rubbish aim. He tried to whack me with the gun instead of firing it."

"Not only that, but his udder-acid was not powerful enough," said Toro.

"Ow!" said Bo, holding her own udder in sympathy.

"We have made the mark-two moo-tants much more powerful," Toro went on. "Sharper. More aggressive. And much, *much* hungrier."

"Huh," said Gipsy. "As if carnivores needed bigger appetites."

"But they *do*," rasped the Raptor Royal. "Because the new moo-tantssss will eat nothing but plantssss! Fernssss, grassssss, trees, bushes — they will devour them all . . ."

Suddenly, Teggs groaned. "I just remembered! After our first battle with the moo-tant, Admiral Rosso told us that one thousand tons of long grass had been stolen from Mossmunch II."

Gipsy glared at the Raptor Royal. "That was down to you?"

"Of course," said Toro. "We had to develop our moo-tants' appetites . . ."

Bo was puzzled. "But if the moo-tants don't want to eat other animals, that makes your army *less* dangerous . . . doesn't it?"

"Savagery alone is not the answer," said Toro. "Not only will the new moo-tants invade the Vegetarian Sector with awesome power, they will eat every single plant they come across . . ."

Teggs was appalled. "That means that as they spread through our side of space, all plant-eating dinos will starve to death!"

"Exactly," hissed the Raptor Royal. "Instead of fighting to the end, your kind will be forced to leave the Jurassic Quadrant just to feed themselves – so we meat-eaters can move in and take over your territory."

141

"That's monstrous!" shouted Teggs. McMoo and Gipsy nodded angrily.

Bo was so angry she shot a super-sized jet of milk from her udder at Toro. He ducked, and the milk splashed over the controls instead; they steamed and fizzled.

The Raptor Royal hissed angrily. "Do that again, cow, and you will die at once."

"Why did you come so far to cause this carnage, Toro?" Gipsy demanded.

"Just what exactly will the Raptor Royal do for you in return?"

The Raptor Royal grinned and held up a round silver disc.

The Cows In Action groaned loudly.

"An F.B.I. time machine," said McMoo. "You're going to bring that monster back to Earth with you?"

"Not alone. I shall attach time machines to a whole fleet of flying saucers." Toro smiled, staring into the distance, imagining the chaos to come. "Soon, an army of carnivore dinosaurs, led by *me*, will travel back one million years through space and time to drop in on the prehistoric planet Earth. Early humans will feed my hungry, hunting hordes. Then the dinosaurs will depart and I shall take my rightful place as ruler of all cattle . . . We will build a cow civilization that will stretch around the globe. Humankind will never have existed – *cows will rule the Earth!*"

143

"Except they won't," said the Raptor Royal gruffly. "Because we dinosaurs will not sssstop at eating humans. We will eat all other animals on Earth too – even COWS!"

Toro whirled round to stare at him. "Huh?"

"Earth was *our* planet, fool," the Raptor Royal went on. "We will devour every living thing – what exotic sssssnacksss to enjoy! Not just in prehistoric times, but in *all* times . . ." With a swipe of his battle-scarred tail, he pushed Toro down the steps. The buffalo landed flat on his snout in the arena.

Teggs hauled Toro back to his hooves. "You crazy idiot! You've handed the most ruthless meat-eating monster in the universe the secret of time travel *and* safe passage to Earth."

"Indeed he has." Chuckling, the Raptor Royal carefully put down the time disc. "And now I shall hand you all over to the new, improved dinosaur moo-tantsss."

"More kidnapped T. rex miners?" sneered Gipsy.

"Of course not! I only used those T. rexes because I did not wish to risk raptor warriors in an untested experiment." The regal monster crossed to a control panel that had escaped Bo's milk-attack. "Now the processsss is perfected, we have moo-tated an entire army of prime raptors here in my underground labs! And what better time to test them out than right now?"

The Raptor Royal pressed a button, and a cavernous split opened up in the far wall of the arena. A wave of heat warmed the subterranean space, and stinking yellow steam floated out of the gap.

The shuffle and stomp of heavy feet signalled the coming of at least fifty super-scary-looking raptors! Their scaly bodies were lumpy with muscles. Sharp horns curled out of their heads. Vast udders bulged from their bellies. Grass and hay spilled from their sharp jaws, and they clutched diabolical dairy-weapons in their claws. *ZZAP! Ka-SQUELCH!* The moo-tant raptors ruthlessly gunned down the C. rex guards with torrents of killer cream-cheese and yoghurt, then kept on coming . . .

Toro sank to his knees at the sight of his creations coming to get him, while Teggs, Gipsy, Bo and McMoo huddled together as the creatures fanned out, advancing on their prey.

Gipsy struck a dino-judo pose. "It looks like we're going down."

"Yes, it does." Teggs raised his spiky tail. "But let's go down fighting."

"To the last breath, Captain." Professor

McMoo lowered his head, ready to lock horns with the monsters. "It's been an honour to know you all."

"You said it, Prof!" Bo blew a gum bubble and shoved out her udder. "Now, if these creeps want a final battle, I say ... *BRING IT ON!*"

With an ear-splitting roar, the dinosaur moo-tants crowded forward to attack ...

Chapter Twelve

THE BREW OF FREEDOM

Suddenly, an enormous wave of blazing butter burst across the arena with

ferocious force. It broke over the raptor moo-tants and drove them back, slipping and sliding, falling and squalling . . .

Teggs blinked. "Where did all that butter come from?"

Like McMoo, Bo and Gipsy, he turned in the direction of the blast –

to see Pat and Iggy standing by the exit, each cradling an enormous smoking butter-bazooka!

"Excuse me," said Pat, beaming. "Are we in the right place for a last-minute rescue?"

"What is thisss?" screeched the Raptor Royal. "Curse you, milk-cow. Your milk blew up my early warning ssssystem!"

"Yay, me!" Bo cheered. "And, yay, Pat and Jiggy!"

"*Iggy* beefed up the butter-bazookas," Pat explained. The cow-dinos in the steaming sludge were starting to get up, so he fired another extreme stream in their direction. "Sixteen times the firepower!"

"Fancy a closer look?" Iggy turned his own bazooka on the Raptor Royal and let rip with a whopping butter-barrage that swept the king off his clawed feet. The raptor's crown fell off as he went sloshing over the steps, and he slid about desperately trying to grab it.

"Fantastic work, Ig!" cheered Teggs. "You too, Pat!" He rushed over to join them in the mouth of the tunnel, Gipsy and Bo close behind him.

"Wait for me," said McMoo, forcing Toro ahead of him.

Bo frowned. "What are you bothering with him for?"

"Toro and those monsters deserve each other," Iggy agreed.

"He created the moo-tants," McMoo reminded them. "We need him to help us *un*-create them."

"Never!" snarled Toro.

"Really?" Teggs stretched out his tail and lifted the buffalo into the air. "Then maybe we should throw you back to those things?"

Toro stared at the mass of scaly, scrabbling moo-tant monsters in the pool of yellow slime – and then his eyes rolled back into his head and he went limp in Teggs's grip.

"He fainted!" Bo groaned. "So much for the leader of the F.B.I."

Gipsy snorted. "What a mega-wuss!"

Teggs turned to Iggy and Pat. "Is Arx minding the *Sauropod*?"

"No, Alass is," said Pat. "Arx is waiting outside. Sprite brought us all down in the shuttle."

"You're DOWN to your last five minutesss of life, you plant-gobbling guppies!" The Raptor Royal had reclaimed his crown, but it was dripping goo all down his face. "Up, dino moo-tantsss!" he

154

raged. "Get up and crunch our enemies! *Ssscrunch* them!"

Rallied by their raptor lord, the moo-tants got messily to their feet.

"Quick," said McMoo. "Give them another butter-blast!"

"Er . . ." Iggy squeezed the trigger, but only a small splurge fell sizzling from the nozzle. "The only trouble with sixteen times the firepower is that you run out of butter sixteen times as quickly."

"You mean there's no more ammo?" cried Bo in dismay.

"Then it's time to go," said Teggs as the moo-tants began splashing towards them. "Come on!"

The six friends ran for their lives through the dark, dank tunnels, Teggs dragging Toro behind him. The clatter of angry monster raptors echoed scarily behind them.

Finally, they emerged into daylight, where the roar of the wild sea was almost drowned out by the throaty jets of the *Sauropod*'s Shuttle Alpha, high overhead. The cold air was salty and sharp.

"Bracing, isn't it?" said McMoo. "Great spot for a picnic — if it wasn't for all the killer moo-tant monsters about the place." He frowned when he saw Arx waiting for them with the big box of Plurge tea bags balanced on his horns. "Hey, big fella! Did you read my mind? A brew would be heaven right now."

"I'm afraid we can't use them yet," said Arx. "Are there moo-tants close behind you?"

"*Too* close!" Gipsy ran up and hugged him. "Oh, it's good to see you, Arx!"

"It certainly is," Teggs agreed. "Now, let's get out of here."

Arx shook his head. "We can't, Captain. First, we have to lure those moo-tants into the sea." Balancing the box, he galloped over to the cliff edge, high above the stormy ocean. "We must all stand here, so that they charge straight at us."

Teggs stared at him. "Have you gone space crazy, Arx?"

"It's the only way we can beat those things," Pat insisted. He and Iggy dropped in the guns, picked up two enormous jars of pale liquid from beside the saucer, and went to stand beside Arx. "Trust us!"

"That goes without saying," McMoo

murmured, following them to the precipice. Teggs nodded too, dragging Toro over to join the line.

"What's in the jars, boys?" asked Gipsy as she and Bo joined the crowd.

But before she could get an answer, the dinosaur moo-tants burst out of the tunnel, shrieking and roaring – a seething bundle of buttery belligerence. Within seconds the monsters were racing towards the astrosaurs, udders bubbling, dairy-weapons dripping – an awe-inspiring mass of scaly, destructive doom.

Bo put her hoof up in the air. "I have a question," she said. "Now those nightmares are charging straight for us . . . what are we going to do?"

"JUMP!" chorused Arx, Pat and Iggy. They turned and leaped off the ledge, landing in the frothing sea with a joint, colossal *SPLASH*. Their enormous jars quickly sank from sight, the contents washing away into the surrounding water.

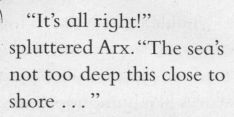

"It's all right!" spluttered Arx. "The sea's not too deep this close to shore . . ."

Quickly, Teggs threw himself and Toro over the edge. *SPLOSH!*

"Geronimoooooooo!" cried Bo, diving into the choppy blood-red ocean with Gipsy and Professor McMoo. *SPLASH! SPLUSH! PLOP!*

Unable to stop their charge, the dinosaur moo-tants went blundering over the precipice, crashing into the waves like humongous missiles.

"Incoming!" McMoo gargled, covering his head as monsters rained down around them.

"Well done, all!" yelled Arx, watching Iggy and Pat scattering the tea bags from the box all around them.

"Quickly, everyone," Teggs spluttered, trying to keep Toro afloat as cow-dinos roared and thrashed in the water around them. "Get to shore!"

"Good plan," said McMoo, swimming while trying to hold his glasses in place. "Certainly a better plan than throwing away my lovely tea bags! I don't know what you're up to, Arx, but I could murder a cuppa."

"Sprite's on the case, Professor," Arx replied as Shuttle Alpha began to drop out of the sky. "Here he comes . . ."

"This had better work," cried Pat, "or we're sunk!"

"In more ways than one," Iggy agreed, paddling for his life.

The shuttle hovered over the surface of the sea as though trying to land. Its jets flared and belched fire. The sea-water around them began to bubble.

"Hey!" called Bo, ducking the swipe of a moo-tant's claws. "It's getting like a hot tub around here."

"A *too*-hot tub!" Teggs agreed as a familiar smell filled the air.

"Ugh!" Gipsy tried to hold her nose while wading through the water. "That pondy pong is back."

"Hot fresh Plurge!" McMoo realized, helping Teggs drag Toro through the waves. "Pat, Arx, Iggy – you're using the shuttle's jets to turn the sea water into *tea* water!"

"Right!" Pat agreed, splashing out of the hot, steamy stew. "I guessed that the magic ingredient in the moo-tant transformation was that Amazon herb with the special properties."

"It's a wonder-herb, Professor," said Arx, smiling in the surf. "When I added some warm tea-bag juice to that cure we concocted, it turned the C. rex back to normal. It works!"

"And that cure was in the jars we were carrying," Iggy explained, helping Bo out onto the rocky shore. "With any luck, now that we've mixed everything together and warmed it up nicely too—"

"It's happening!" Bo bellowed as the shuttle lifted off again, high into the sky. "The moo-tants are turning back to normal. You can see it happening as you watch!"

It was true. The monsters were losing their horns, their tails and their big bulging udders, returning to their rotten raptor selves.

The waves carried them along and crashed them down on the rocky beach.

Teggs grinned. "Looks like the moo-tants are all washed up!"

Gipsy still looked worried. "Er, raptors are still kind of dangerous . . ."

"These ones won't be," Arx assured her. "A side effect of the cure is that the patient falls into a deep sleep."

"There you go!" McMoo beamed around at his friends. "Whenever you've got problems, a nice cup of tea will always help!"

"It'll take more than that to sort out the Raptor Boil," said Bo, picking up

a yoghurt cannon from the surf. "*Royal*, I mean . . . Like the right royal pasting I'm going to give him!"

"Little Bo's right," said Teggs, picking up Toro once more — and an abandoned cream pistol. "That carnivore king plotted the doom of the entire Vegetarian Sector. We have to bring him to justice."

The others grabbed washed-up weapons and quickly scaled the rocky cliff face, climbing back towards the entrance of the arena. They found the Raptor Royal looking down from the top of the precipice and hopping with rage.

"My ssssinister grasssss-eating army is undone!" he snarled. "How can thisss be? Those pathetic plant-eaters can't have beaten the great Raptor Royal!"

"I think you'll find we have!" cried Teggs, dropping Toro on the ground. "And now we've *caught* you too."

The big, blubbery raptor spun round to face them, his eyes narrowing with hate.

"Hold it!" Gipsy aimed her sour-cream squirter. "Try to escape, and we'll turn your army's weapons back on you – extremely hard."

"I think not." The Raptor Royal pulled the F.B.I. time-travel disc out from under his robes and jumped on top of it. "Thanksss to Toro, I can escape through time—"

"No!" Teggs and McMoo started forward to try and grab him. But the Raptor Royal was already disappearing in a haze of black smoke. Gipsy fired a volley of sizzling sour cream, but it passed straight through the ruler's ghostly image.

McMoo shook his head. "It's too late. We can't stop him now."

A low snigger from ground level warned them that Toro had woken up — and he seemed to like the view. "No one can stop that raptor," he muttered. "Not even himself!"

The black smoke was turning green. The carnivore started to flicker and blur like a bad TV picture. "What . . . is . . . happening?" he groaned.

"I planned to betray you, Raptor — just as you betrayed me!" Toro shouted. "I booby-trapped your time machine to get rid of you when your usefulness was ended. It will fling you millions of years into the future and then self-destruct!"

"No!" moaned the Raptor Royal, fading away like a ghost. "You can't do thisss to me . . ."

"He didn't." Teggs grinned. "You did it

to yourself."

Pat waved. "So long, sucker!"

There was a loud *POP!*, a small, sooty explosion – and the Raptor Royal vanished.

"He's . . . gone," Arx murmured.

"*Vanished*," Iggy agreed, stunned by what he'd seen.

"Uh-oh," said Gipsy, pointing behind them. "Toro's attempting his own disappearing act!"

With his enemies distracted, the buffalo had seized his chance and was running for the nearest saucer.

"Don't think so!" said Bo. She let rip with her yoghurt cannon, while Teggs fired his cream pistol. The combined blast knocked Toro off his hooves and slammed him into the side of the saucer. He collapsed in a heap, unconscious again – and Teggs and Bo high-fived.

"The menace of the moo-tants is over," breathed Gipsy. "It's *really* over!"

Pat nodded in a daze. "We've brought

down all the bad guys."

"I can't quite believe it," said Arx.

"Seeing is believing, big fella," said McMoo, a smile spreading over his face – the biggest smile Pat had ever seen. "Although on this occasion, '*sea*ing is *tea-leaf*ing'!"

Everyone groaned at the professor's awful joke. But the groans soon turned to laughter – joyful laughter that carried over the roar of the waves to where Shuttle Alpha still hovered, and beyond, all the way to the distant stars above.

Epilogue

FAREWELLS

"Well, then!" said Teggs at last. "That seems to be just about everything wrapped up."

"Yes," McMoo agreed. "The F.B.I.'s greatest ever plan has been foiled."

Arx stared down at the sleeping scaly figures on the beach. "The Raptor Royal has been defeated and the dinosaur moo-tants returned to normal . . ."

"And losing their rulers should leave the raptors in a right royal mess," said Gipsy. "I bet they won't be dreaming up any more invasions for a while."

Bo sat down heavily on Toro's stomach,

squashing him into the ground. "As if that wasn't enough, we've captured the Head Bull of the F.B.I. . . .'

"And stopped him from changing history," Pat added. "Both here and back on Earth."

"And we've met each other too," said Teggs. "Two groups of friends, fighting evil, millions of light years apart . . ."

"It's been a meeting I'll never forget," said McMoo with a smile.

"We won't, either," said Gipsy, and the other astrosaurs nodded.

"After all, we've got enough bumps and bruises to remind us for months!" joked Iggy.

"Just don't forget to take Toro with you when you go," said Arx.

"We'll stow him aboard our flying saucer," McMoo assured him, "ready to face the justice of the C.I.A."

"Could you possibly tow his saucer behind you?" asked Teggs. "Then you could use it to send that kidnapped torvosaurus back here where she belongs."

"Good plan," said the professor. "I'll leave it pre-programmed – once you've taken care of her, you can send T-5 back to us."

"Captain, you are so thoughtful," said Iggy, "worrying about Cindy the big-bummed carnivore like that."

"It's only thanks to her that we got into the Carnivore Sector at all," Teggs reminded him.

"Eep!" came a plaintive call from Shuttle Alpha above.

"Sorry, Sprite, you're right!" Gipsy shouted up to him. "The dimorphodon's needlework played a vital part too!"

Sprite waved and nodded happily.

"Now, it's time we got aboard that shuttle and

zipped back to the *Sauropod*," Teggs
declared. "We can't risk being found here
in meat-eater space."

"No, of course not." McMoo looked
fondly at Teggs. Then he
saluted. "Cheerio then,
Captain."

Teggs gave him a
crooked smile. "Look
after the Earth for us,
won't you? Don't let
those funny human
things muck it up!"

"We'll try." Pat
shook Teggs's paw
while Bo settled
for half strangling
the stegosaurus with
an ultra-tight hug. She
then grabbed Gipsy and Arx in a warm
embrace, and kissed Iggy on the cheek.

"Actually, could I ask for something?"
asked Iggy.

Bo fluttered her eyelids. "My hoof in marriage?"

"Er, no." Iggy smiled. "A couple of cowpats, if possible."

"Oh," said Bo.

"Y'see, the *Sauropod* will have to move pretty fast to get back past the Raptor Border Patrol," Iggy explained, "and your dung drives an engine like nothing I've seen!"

"Well, I left one over there by the entrance when those moo-tants came out," Pat confessed. "Help yourself!"

McMoo sniffed. "And from the smell of things, when you blasted Toro, he dropped enough dirties to see you all the way home in no time."

Gipsy grinned. "Nice of him to try and make amends like that!"

"Isn't it?" said Teggs. "Safe journey, Professor – you too, Pat and Bo. Perhaps, one day, we will meet again."

"You could be right," McMoo agreed. "I'm sure you have no end of adventures out here – and we can't let you have all the fun, can we?"

"Luckily, you're not too far away from us by flying saucer," said Pat. "If you need us, give us a shout."

Teggs nodded. "And if you ever need help with a crisis in history . . . ?"

"We'll get straight on the time-telephone, Cap'n!" Bo assured him. "So long!"

The professor and Pat followed Bo as she dragged Toro into their saucer. "I wonder if we can stop off mid-voyage for a cuppa?" McMoo wondered. "There's bound to be a nice intergalactic café somewhere in the Milky Way . . ."

With a final cheery wave, he closed the spaceship's battered door.

Teggs waved back, then whistled up to Sprite. "All right, down you come! It's time for us to go too."

Just a couple of minutes later, Shuttle Alpha touched down in thick clouds of smoke. Iggy completed his cowpat collection, and the saucer took off, dragging Toro's spacecraft silently behind. Within seconds, both vessels had vanished into the clouds.

"There go the Cows In Action," said Gipsy. "Back to Earth, and more adventures."

"I wonder just how long their journey will take?" mused Arx.

"I think they'll *always* be journeying," said Teggs. "Through the past, present and future."

"And what about our future?" wondered Iggy. "What's next?"

"For us?" Teggs beamed round at his friends. "Why, even more action and excitement in outer space, of course.

Wild, crazy adventures are what
our lives are all about – and
always will be!"

From the bestselling author of

Astrosaurs and **Cows In Action**

THE SLIME SQUAD

vs

THE FEARSOME FISTS

STEVE COLE

Read on, but remember –

IF YOU CAN'T TAKE THE SLIME, DON'T DO THE CRIME!

ONCE UPON A SLIME...

The old rubbish dump was a long way from anywhere. It stretched out as far as the eye could see – a mucky, dusty, smelly, rusty landscape of thousands of thrown-away things.

It had been closed for years. Abandoned. Forgotten.

Nobody ever came here. Few people even knew it existed. So there was no one around to wonder who had built the slightly crooked house beside the rubbish dump – or to ask why they had moved away again in such a hurry. There was no one around at all.

Apart from . . . the MONSTERS!

There were thousands of them living here. Millions, maybe. Bright and bold and curious creatures no bigger than a finger, who did not think of the old rubbish dump as a rubbish dump at all.

To them it was a whole wide and wonderful world of whiffy possibilities. They called it *Trashland*.

These miniature monsters didn't know where they had come from. They didn't know *what* they had come from, and they certainly didn't know why.

But they knew that now they were here, they wanted to make the most of it.

So with knowledge they found in thrown-away human books, they got busy inventing the things they needed. They built villages, towns and cities. They worked hard at monster jobs and played hard at monster hobbies.

As the years went by, Trashland became a bustling, happy place where the little monsters lived in peace and where crime was almost unheard of.

And then, one day . . .

Chapter One

A SHAGGY PLOG STORY

Plog the monster woke up in his soggy
shoebox home. Sunlight streamed
through a big crack in the sewer pipe
where the shoebox had washed up long
ago. It looked like a lovely morning.

Plog stretched and yawned
and thought: *What
shall I do today?*
"Same as
every day,"
he mumbled,
climbing
out of
bed.

"I'll watch smellyvision on my own till it's time to go to sleep again."

Scratching his bottom, Plog splashed through the puddles on the floor towards the smellyvision set. He was quite big by miniature monster standards – an orange, bear-shaped animal with a rat-like snout, extra-long ears, a furry tail, tangled whiskers, stripy pyjama bottoms and a grubby brown waistcoat. They were the only clothes Plog owned. But since he never went further than the sewer pipe and no one ever came to visit, it didn't really matter.

"I wish I could go out and make friends and have some fun. I'm fed up with being stuck down here on my own." Plog glanced down at his feet, and shuddered. "But if the ordinary monsters found out my terrible secret, they'd laugh and shout and call me names and drive me out of town . . ."

Just as Plog reached the smellyvision set, his stomach rumbled noisily. *ROARRRR! Blub-bub-bub-GRRRRRRR.* He sighed. He couldn't afford proper food because he didn't have a job. Instead, he ate whatever meals he could put together from stuff he found in the broken sewer pipe – mostly rat hairs and flies' legs in seagull-poo sauce, which tasted pretty horrid but at least stopped his tum from rumbling.

"I'd better go out and find some breakfast," Plog muttered, pushing open his soggy cardboard door and wading into the cold, whiffy water.

PLOG IS IN FOR A SURPRISE!
TO FIND OUT WHAT IT IS, READ

SLIME SQUAD vs THE FEARSOME FISTS

NOW!